NICHOLAS NICKLEBY

NICHOLAS NICKLEBY

Charles Dickens

Bloomsbury Books
London

This edition published 1994 by Bloomsbury Books, an imprint of The Godfrey Cave Group, 42 Bloomsbury Street, London, WC1B 3QJ.

ISBN 1 85471 233 0

Printed and bound by Firmin-Didot (France), Group Herissey. No d'impression : 28013.

Contents

1

A Tempting Offer

Mr Ralph Nickleby lived in a large, handsomely furnished house in Golden Square, which, in addition to a brass plate upon the street door, had another brass plate two sizes and a half smaller upon the left-hand doorpost, displaying the word OFFICE.

The tradesmen thought that he was a sort of lawyer, and the neighbours thought that he was a kind of general agent, and all believed him to be immensely rich.

But Mr Ralph Nickleby was neither a lawyer nor a general agent. He was a usurer, which means a money-lender who lends money at an enormous rate of interest, and more than the law permits.

He sat in his private office one morning ready dressed to walk abroad, wearing a bottle-green spencer, or short over-jacket, over a blue coat, a white waistcoat, grey-mixture pantaloons, and Wellington boots drawn over them.

Mr Nickleby closed an account-book which byon his desk, and, throwing himself back in his chair, gazed through a dirty little window on the left, through which the face of his clerk could be dimly seen.

The clerk was a sallow-faced man in rusty brown,

who sat upon an uncommonly hard stool in a kind of butler's pantry at the end of the passage, and always had a pen behind his ear when he answered the bell. As Mr Nickleby looked through the window, the clerk happened to look up, and Mr Nickleby beckoned him to attend.

In obedience to this summons, the clerk got off the stool, and presented himself in his master's room. He was a tall man, of middle age, with two goggle eyes, a red nose, a thin face, and a suit of clothes much the worse for wear, with so few buttons left upon it, that it was marvellous how he managed to keep the suit on.

"I am going to the London Tavern this morning," said Mr Nickleby.

"Public meeting?" inquired Noggs.

Mr Nickleby nodded. I expect a letter from the solicitor about that mortgage of Ruddle's. If it comes at all, it will be here by the two o'clock delivery. I shall leave the City about that time, and walk to Charing Cross on the left-hand side of the way. If there are any letters, come and meet me, and bring them with you."

Noggs nodded; and as he nodded, there came a ring at the office bell. The clerk went to the door, and presently returned, ushering in a gentle violent hurry.

"My dear Nickleby," said the gentleman, "there's not a moment to lose. I have a cab at the door. Sir Matthew Pupker takes the chair. By-the-bye, what a *very* remarkable man that clerk of yours is."

"Yes, poor devil!" replied Mr Nickleby, drawing on his gloves. "Though Newman Noggs kept his horses and hounds once."

"Ay, ay?" said the other carelessly.

"Yes," continued Ralph Nickleby, "and not many years ago either. But he squandered his money, making first a thorough fool of himself, and then a beggar. He took to drinking, and had a touch of paralysis, and then came here to borrow a pound. And as I wanted a clerk just then, to open the door—and so forth, I took him out of charity, and he has remained with me ever since."

Mr Nickleby did not add that Newman Noggs being utterly poverty-stricken, served him for rather less than the usual wages of a boy of thirteen.

But the other gentleman was plainly impatient to be gone; and as they hurried into the hackney cab, perhaps Mr Nickleby forgot to mention so unimportant a thing.

The public meeting being over, Ralph Nickleby bent his steps westward. As he passed St. Paul's Cathedral, he stepped aside into a doorway to set his watch, when a man suddenly stopped before him. It was Newman Noggs

"Ah! Newman," said Mr Nickleby, "the letter about the mortgage has come, has it? I thought it would."

"Wrong," replied Newman.

"What! And nobody called respecting it?"

Noggs shook his head.

"What has come, then?" inquired Mr Nickleby.

"I have," said Newman.

"What else?" demanded his master sternly.

"This," said Newman, drawing a sealed letter slowly from his pocket. "Postmark, Strand; black wax, black border, woman's hand, C. N. in the corner."

"Black wax?" said Mr Nickleby, glancing at the letter.

"I know something of that hand, too. Newman, I shouldn't be surprised if my brother were dead." And, snatching the letter from his clerk, Ralph opened it, read it, put it in his pocket, and began winding up his watch.

"It is as I expected, Newman," said Mr Nickleby. "He *is* dead. Dear me! Well, that's a sudden thing." And, replacing his watch in his fob, he walked slowly westward, with his hands behind him.

"Children alive?" inquired Newman, stepping up to him.

"Why, that's the very thing," replied Mr Nickleby. "They are both alive."

"Both!" repeated Newman Noggs, in a low voice.

"And the widow, too," added Mr Nickleby; "and all three in London—confound them! All three here, Newman."

Newman fell a little behind his master, and his face was curiously twisted, as by a spasm, but whether of paralysis, or of grief, or of inward laughter, nobody but himself could possibly explain.

"Go home!" said Ralph Nickleby, after they had walked a few paces, looking round at the clerk as if he were a dog.

The words were scarcely uttered, when Newman darted across the road, slunk among the crowd, and disappeared in an instant.

"Reasonable, certainly" muttered Mr Nickleby to himself, as he walked on. "My brother never did anything for me, and I never expected it. The breath is no sooner out of his body than I am to be looked to as the support of a great hearty woman and a grown boy and girl. What are they to me? *I* never saw them."

Full of these thoughts, Mr Nickleby made his way to the Strand, and, stopping at a private door about half-way down the crowded thoroughfare, gave a double knock, which was answered by a servant-girl, with an uncommonly dirty face.

"Is Mrs Nickleby at home, girl?" demanded Ralph sharply.

"Her name ain't Nickleby," said the girl. "La Creevy you mean."

"It's the second floor, Hannah," cried a female voice from the staircase. "What a stupid thing you are. Show the gentleman where the bell is, and tell him he mustn't knock double knocks for the second floor."

"Here," said Ralph, walking in without more ado, "I beg your pardon. Is that Mrs La What's-her-name ?"

"Creevy—La Creevy," replied the voice, as a yellow head-dress bobbed over the banisters.

"I gather from what you said to your servant, ma'am," said Mr Nickleby, walking up the stairs, "that the floor above belongs to you."

"Yes, it does," Miss La Creevy replied, and added that she was in the habit of letting it. Indeed, there was a lady from the country with her two children in the rooms now.

"A widow, ma'am?" said Ralph.

"Yes, she is a widow," replied Miss La Creevy.

"A *poor* widow, ma'am?" asked Mr Nickleby.

"Well, I'm afraid she *is* poor," rejoined Miss La Creevy.

"I happen to know that she is, ma'am," said Ralph.

"Now, what business has a poor widow in such a house as this? I know her circumstances, ma'am; in fact, I am a relation of the family; and I should not recommend you to keep them here, ma'am. How long have they taken these lodgings for?"

"Only from week to week," replied Miss La Creevy. "Mrs Nickleby paid the first week in advance."

"Then you had better get them out at the end of it," said Ralph. "They can't do better than go back to the country, ma'am. They are in everybody's way here."

"I have nothing whatever to say against the lady," said Miss La Creevy, "though, poor thing, she seems terribly low in her spirits; nor against the young people either, for nicer or better-behaved young people cannot be."

"Very well, ma'am," said Ralph; "I have done my duty. Good-morning. Now for my sister-in-law." And, climbing up the other flight of stairs, Mr Nickleby stopped to take breath on the landing, when he was overtaken by the handmaid, whom Miss La Creevy had despatched to announce him.

"What name?" said the girl.

"Nickleby," replied Ralph.

"Oh! Mrs Nickleby," said the girl, throwing open the door, "here's Mr Nickleby."

A lady in deep mourning rose as Ralph Nickleby entered, and put her hand upon the arm of a very beautiful girl of about seventeen. A youth, who appeared a year or two older, stepped forward, and saluted Ralph as his uncle.

"Oh!" growled Ralph, with an ill-favoured frown, "you are Nicholas, I suppose?"

"That is my name, sir," replied the youth.

"Put my hat down," said Ralph imperiously. "Well, ma'am, how do you do? You must bear up against sorrow, ma'am. I always do."

"Mine was no common loss!" said Mrs Nickleby, putting her handkerchief to her eyes.

"It was no uncommon loss, ma'am," returned Ralph, as he coolly unbuttoned his spencer. "Husbands die every day, ma'am, and wives also."

"And brothers also, sir," said Nicholas, with a glance of indignation.

"Yes, sir, and puppies, and pug-dogs likewise," replied his uncle, taking a chair. "You didn't mention in your letter what my brother's complaint was, ma'am."

"We have too much reason to fear that he died of a broken heart," said Mrs Nickleby, shedding tears; for Nicholas's father had speculated with his little fortune, and had lost it all.

"Pooh!" said Ralph. "There's no such thing as a broken heart. If a man can't pay his debts, he dies, you say, of a broken heart, and his widow's a martyr."

"Some people, I believe, have no hearts to break," said Nicholas quietly.

"How old is this boy, for Heaven's sake?" inquired Ralph, wheeling back his chair, and surveying his nephew from head to foot with the greatest scorn.

"Nicholas is very nearly nineteen," replied the widow.

"Nineteen, eh?" said Ralph. "And what do you mean to do for your bread, sir?"

"Not to live upon my mother," replied Nicholas, his breast swelling as he spoke.

"You'd have little enough to live upon if you did," retorted his uncle, eyeing him contemptuously.

"Whatever it be," said Nicholas, flushed with anger, "I shall not look to you to make it more."

"Nicholas, my dear, recollect yourself," said Mrs Nickleby.

"Hold your tongue, sir!" said Ralph. "Upon my word! Fine beginnings, Mrs Nickleby—fine beginnings!"

Mrs Nickleby made a sign to Nicholas to keep silent; and the uncle and nephew looked at each other for some seconds without speaking. The face of the old man was stern, hard featured, and forbidding; that of the young one, open, handsome, and generous. The old man's eye was keen with avarice and cunning; the young man's, bright with the light of intelligence and spirit.

The sight of the handsome, spirited young fellow galled Ralph to the heart's core; and he hated Nicholas from that hour.

"Boy!" he muttered, with a great show of disdain, and, withdrawing his eyes, he turned to the widow. "And you tell me there is nothing left for you?" he asked.

"Nothing," faltered Mrs Nickleby.

"And you spent what little money you had in coming all the way to London to see what I could do for you?" went on Ralph.

"I hoped," faltered Mrs Nickleby, "that you might have an opportunity of doing something for your brother's children. I—"

"What is your daughter fit for, ma'am?"

"Kate has been well educated," sobbed Mrs Nickleby.

"We must try and get her apprenticed at some boarding school," said Ralph. "Have you ever done anything, sir?" he added, turning to his nephew.

"No," replied Nicholas bluntly.

"No; I thought not!" said Ralph. "This is the way my brother brought up his children, ma'am."

"Nicholas has not long completed his education," rejoined Mrs Nickleby, "and he was thinking of—

"The old story," interrupted Ralph. "Always thinking, and never doing. Are you willing to work, sir?" he inquired, frowning on his nephew.

"Of course I am," replied Nicholas haughtily.

"Then, see here, sir," said his uncle. "This caught my eye this morning, and you may thank your stars for it." With that he took a newspaper from his pocket, and, after unfolding it, read as follows:—

EDUCATION.—At Mr Wackford Squeers's Academy, Dotheboys Hall—at the delightful village of Dotheboys, near Greta Bridge in Yorkshire— Youth are boarded, clothed, booked, furnished with pocket-money, instructed in all languages, mathematics, orthography, astronomy, the use of the globes, algebra, writing, arithmetic, and every other branch of classical literature. Terms, twenty guineas per annum. No extras, and no vacations. Mr Squeers is in town, and attends daily, from one to four, at the Saracen's Head, Snow Hill. N. B.—An able assistant wanted. Annual salary, £5—A Master of Arts would be preferred'

"There!" said Ralph, folding the paper again. "Let him get that situation, and his fortune is made. Without friends, money, or knowledge of business of any kind, he won't find honest employment in London which will keep him in shoe-leather."

"Sir," said Nicholas, after thinking awhile, "if I am fortunate enough to be appointed to this post, for which I am so imperfectly qualified, what will become of those I leave behind?"

"Your mother and sister, sir," replied Ralph, "will be provided for in that case—not otherwise—by me, and placed in some sphere of life in which they will be able to be independent."

"Then," said Nicholas, starting gaily up and wringing his uncle's hand, "I am ready to do anything you wish me. Let us try our fortune with Mr Squeers at once. He can but refuse."

"He won't do that," said Ralph. "He will be glad to have you on my recommendation. Make yourself of use to him, and you'll rise to be a partner in the establishment in no time."

Again Nicholas shook his uncle's hand, and, having carefully copied the address of Mr Squeers, the uncle and nephew sallied forth together in quest of that accomplished gentleman.

"I am sure your uncle is a much more kindly-disposed person than he looks," said Mrs Nickleby to Kate.

"He might easily be, mamma," answered Kate.

2

The Yorkshire Schoolmaster

In the coffee-room of the inn known as the Saracen's Head, Mr Wackford Squeers stood with his hands in his pockets. Mr Squeers had but one eye, and that eye was of a greenish-grey colour, in shape resembling the fan-light of a street door.

The blind side of his face was much wrinkled and puckered up, which gave him a villainous appearance. His hair was very flat and shiny—save at the ends, where it was brushed stiffly up from a low forehead; and he had a harsh voice and coarse manner.

Mr Squeers was about fifty-two years of age, and a trifle below the middle size. He wore a white neckerchief with long ends and a suit of black; but, his coat sleeves being too long, and his trousers too short, he appeared ill at ease in his clothes.

In a corner of the seat in the coffee-room was a very small deal trunk, tied round with a scanty piece of cord; and on the trunk was perched—his lace-up half-boots and corduroy trousers dangling in the air—a small boy, who, with his shoulders drawn up to his ears, and his hands planted on his knees, glanced timidly at the schoolmaster.

"Half-past three," muttered Mr Squeers, looking sulkily at the coffee-room clock. "There will be nobody here today. At Midsummer I took down ten boys; ten twenties is two hundred pound. What's come of all the boys? What's parents got in their heads?"

Here the little boy on the top of the trunk gave a violent sneeze.

"Hallo, sir!" growled the schoolmaster, turning round. "What's that, sir?"

"Please, sir, I sneezed," answered the little boy, trembling till the trunk shook under him.

"Oh! sneezed, did you?" retorted Mr Squeers. And with that he knocked the boy off the trunk with a blow on one side of the face, and knocked him on again with a blow on the other.

The little boy screwed a couple of knuckles into each of his eyes and began to cry.

"Wait till I get you down to Yorkshire, my young gentleman," said Mr Squeers, "and the—"

"Mr Squeers," said the waiter, looking in, "here's a gentleman asking for you at the bar."

"Show the gentleman in, Richard," replied Mr Squeers in a soft voice. And he added in a fierce whisper, "Put your handkerchief into your pocket, you little scoundrel."

The stranger entered at that moment; but Mr Squeers pretended not to see him, and began to mend a pen. "My dear child," said the schoolmaster aloud, "all people have their trials. You are leaving your friends, but you will have a father in me, my dear, and a mother in Mrs Squeers. At the delightful village of Dotheboys—

Here he was interrupted by the new-comer, who had brought with him two little boys. "Mr Squeers, I believe, sir?" said the stranger.

"The same, sir," said Mr Squeers, looking round with an air of extreme surprise.

"I am in the oil and colour way, sir," said the stranger. "My name is Snawley. I have been thinking, Mr Squeers, of placing my two boys at your school. Could I say a few words with you apart, sir?" and he looked full into Mr Squeers's one eye.

"By all means," rejoined Mr Squeers. "My dears, will you speak to your new playfellow a minute or two?— That is one of my boys, sir. Belling is his name. He goes down with me tomorrow. That's his luggage that he is a-sitting upon now. Each boy is required to bring, sir, two suits of clothes, six shirts, Six pair of stockings, two nightcaps, two pocket-handkerchiefs, two pair of shoes, and two hats."

Mr Snawley was a sleek, flat-nosed man, with a very hypocritical face. And as they stood apart, the schoolmaster whispered, "Let us understand each other, Mr Snawley. I see we may safely do so. Who are these boys?"

"The fact is," said Mr Snawley, "I am their stepfather, Mr Squeers. I have married their mother, sir. And as she has a little money in her own right, I am afraid, Mr Squeers, that she might be led to squander it on them, sir."

"*I* see," returned Mr Squeers.

"And this," went on Mr Snawley, "has made me anxious to put them to some school a good distance off, where there are no holidays.

"The payments regular," interrupted Mr Squeers, "and no questions asked."

"That's it exactly," rejoined the other.

Then Mr Squeers took Mr Snawley's address, and had the agreeable task of writing the receipt for the first quarter's payment in advance, which he had scarcely completed, when another voice was heard inquiring for Mr Squeers.

"Here he is," replied the schoolmaster. "What is it?"

"Only a matter of business, sir," said Ralph Nickleby, presenting himself, closely followed by Nicholas. "There was an advertisement of yours in the papers this morning?"

"There was, sir. This way, if you please," said Mr Squeers. "Won't you be seated?"

"Why, I think I will," replied Ralph, suiting the action to the words. "This is my nephew, sir— Mr Nicholas Nickleby."

Nicholas bowed, and seemed very much astonished at the outward appearance of the head master of Dotheboys Hall.

"Perhaps you recollect me?" said Ralph, looking narrowly at the schoolmaster.

"You paid me a small account at each of my half-yearly visits to London for some years, I think, sir," replied Squeers, "for the parents of a boy named Dorker, who unfortunately—

"Unfortunately died at Dotheboys Hall," said Ralph, finishing the sentence.

"I remember it very well, sir," said Mr Squeers. Then, seeing Ralph looking round at the strangers present, he added, "These are only some pupils of mine who are to be educated at Dotheboys Hall, where youth are boarded, clothed, booked, washed—"

"Yes, we know all about that," interrupted Ralph testily. "Suppose we come to business?"

"With all my heart, sir," said Mr Squeers. "Never postpone business" is the very first lesson we instil into our commercial pupils. Master Belling, my dear, always remember that."

"Yes, sir," replied Master Belling.

"He recollects what it is, does he?" said Ralph

"Tell the gentleman," said Mr Squeers.

"Never," repeated Master Belling.

"Very good," said Mr Squeers. "Go on."

"Never," repeated Master Belling.

"Very good indeed," said Mr Squeers. "Yes."

"P," suggested Nicholas good-naturedly.

"Perform—business!" said Master Belling. "Never — perform business!"

"Very well, sir," said Squeers, darting a withering look at his pupil. "You and I will perform a little business on our private account by-and-by."

"And just now," put in Ralph, "we had better transact our own, perhaps. You have advertised for an able assistant, sir?"

"Precisely so," said Mr Squeers.

"Here he is!" said Ralph. "My nephew Nicholas, fresh from school. He is just the man you want."

"I'm afraid the young man won't suit me," said Squeers, looking in a puzzled way at the gentleman-like figure of Nicholas.

"I fear, sir," put in Nicholas, "that you object to my youth, and to my not being a Master of Arts."

"Look here, Mr Squeers," interrupted Ralph. "This is a lad, or a young man—or whatever you like to call him—of eighteen or nineteen. His father is dead; he is wholly ignorant of the world; he has no money whatever, and wants something to do. I recommend him to this splendid establishment of yours, as an opening which will lead him to fortune, if he turns it to proper account. Do you see that?"

"Everybody must see that," replied Squeers, half imitating the sneer with which Ralph was regarding his unconscious nephew.

"Look at him," continued Ralph, "and think of the use he may be to you in half-a-dozen ways! Isn't that a question for consideration?"

"Yes, it is," said Squeers, answering a nod of Ralph's head with a nod of his own.

"Good," rejoined Ralph. "Let me have two words with you."

The two words were whispered apart. In a couple of minutes Mr Squeers announced that Mr Nicholas Nickleby was, from that moment, thoroughly installed in the office of assistant master of Dotheboys Hall.

"Your uncle's recommendation has done it, Mr Nickleby," said Mr Squeers.

Nicholas, overjoyed at his success, shook his uncle's hand warmly, and could almost have worshipped Squeers upon the spot.

"He is an odd-looking man," thought Nicholas "But

what of that? Doctor Johnson was an odd-looking man—all these bookworms are."

"At eight o'clock tomorrow morning, Mr Nickleby," said Squeers, "the coach starts." For in the days of our story there were no railways, and people travelled on horseback or by coach. "You must be here at a quarter before eight," added Squeers, "as we take these boys with us."

"Certainly, sir," said Nicholas.

"And your fare down I have paid," growled Ralph. "So you'll have nothing to do but to keep yourself warm."

Nicholas felt this unexpected favour so much, that he could scarcely find words to thank his uncle. "I shall never forget this kindness, sir," he said, as they left the Saracen's Head.

"Take care you don't," replied Ralph. "I shall be here in the morning to see you off. You had better go home now, and pack up what you have got to pack. Do you think you could find your way to Golden Square first?"

"Certainly," said Nicholas. "I can easily inquire the way."

"Leave these papers with my clerk, then," said Ralph, producing a small parcel, "and tell him to wait till I come home."

Nicholas cheerfully undertook the errand, and, starting off with all speed, he found Mr Noggs opening the door with a latchkey, as Nicholas reached the steps of Ralph's house.

"These are the papers from my uncle," said Nicholas, "and you're to have the goodness to wait till he comes home, if you please."

"Uncle!" cried Noggs.

"Mr Nickleby," said Nicholas, in explanation.

"Come in," said Newman. He led Nicholas into the passage, and thence into the little pantry at the end of it, and, folding his arms and thrusting his head forward, he scanned Nicholas's face closely.

"There is no answer," said Nicholas.

Noggs did not reply, and still stared hard at Nicholas.

Nicholas could not help smiling at Newman's peculiar appearance. "Have you any commands for me?" he asked.

Noggs shook his head and sighed. Then he drew a long breath, and said hurriedly, that if the young gentleman did not object to tell, he should like to know what his uncle was going to do for him.

Nicholas had not the least objection in the world, and, sitting down, he entered into a glowing description of all the advantages to be gained from his appointment as assistant master at Dotheboys Hall.

"But what's the matter—are you ill?" said Nicholas, suddenly breaking off, as Noggs, after throwing himself into many strange attitudes, thrust his hands under the stool upon which he sat, and cracked his fingerjoints, as if he were snapping all the bones in his hands.

Newman Noggs made no reply, but went on shrugging his shoulders and cracking his fingerjoints, with a strange smile upon his face, staring at Nicholas in a most ghastly manner.

At first Nicholas thought he was in a fit; then he decided that the clerk was drunk, and deemed it prudent to make off at once.

He looked back when he had got the street door open. Newman Noggs was still shrugging his shoulders, and the cracking of his fingers seemed louder than ever.

3

The Journey

Many tears were dropped by the anxious mother and loving sister into Nicholas's trunk; and there was so much to be done, and so little time to do it in, that the preparations for his journey were made mournfully indeed.

The box was packed at last, and after that came supper, and poor Nicholas nearly choked himself by attempting to eat. But he tried to cheer the ladies with a jest or two, and then they parted tearfully for the night.

Nicholas slept well till six next morning, and rose quite brisk and gay. He wrote a few lines in pencil to say the goodbye which he was afraid to pronounce himself, and, laying them with half his scanty stock of money at his sister's door, he shouldered his luggage and crept softly downstairs.

By the time he had found a man to carry his box, it was only seven o'clock; so he walked slowly on till he reached the Saracen's Head, and looked into the coffee-room in search of Mr Squeers.

He found that learned gentleman sitting at breakfast with the three little boys before mentioned, and two others that had turned up by some lucky chance.

Mr Squeers had before him a small measure of coffee, a plate of hot toast, and a cold round of beef; but he was, at that moment, preparing breakfast for the little boys.

"This is two-penn'orth of milk, is it, waiter?" said Mr Squeers, looking down into a large, blue mug.

"That's two-penn'orth, sir," replied the waiter.

"What a rare article milk is, to be sure, in London!" said Mr Squeers, with a sigh. "Just fill that mug up with lukewarm water, William, will you?"

"To the very top, sir?" inquired the waiter. "Why, the milk will be drownded!"

"Never you mind that," said Mr Squeers. "You ordered that thick bread-and-butter for three, did you?"

"Coming directly, sir."

"Conquer your passions, boys, and don't be eager after vittles," said Mr Squeers; and he took a large bite out of the cold beef, and recognised Nicholas.

"Sit down, Mr Nickleby," said Squeers. "Here we are, a-breakfasting, you see."

Nicholas did *not* see that any one was breakfasting, except Mr Squeers; but he bowed with becoming reverence.

"Oh! that's the milk-and-water, is it, William?" said Squeers. "Very good. Don't forget the bread-and-butter."

At this fresh mention of bread-and-butter the five little boys looked very eager, and followed the waiter out with their eyes. Meanwhile, Mr Squeers tasted the milk-and-water.

"Ah!" said Mr Squeers, smacking his lips, "here's richness! Think of the many beggars and orphans in the streets that would be glad of this, little boys. When I say Number One," went on Mr Squeers, putting the mug before the children, "the boy on the left hand nearest the window may take a drink, and when I say Number Two, the boy next him will go in, and so we will come to Number Five, which is the last boy. Are you ready?"

"Yes, sir," cried all the little boys, with great eagerness.

"Thank God for a good breakfast," said Mr Squeers, when he had finished his own. "Number One may take a drink."

Number One seized the mug ravenously, and had just drunk enough to make him wish for more, when Mr Squeers gave the signal for Number Two, who gave it up, at the same interesting moment, to Number Three; and so on till the mug was emptied by Number Five.

"And now," said the schoolmaster, dividing the bread-and-butter for three into five portions, "you had better look sharp with your breakfast, for the horn will blow in a minute or two."

In a very short time indeed the horn was heard; and Mr Squeers jumped up and produced a little basket from under the seat. "Put what you haven't had time to eat in here, boys!" he said. "You'll want it on the road."

Nicholas was considerably startled at all he had seen and heard; but he had no time to think about it, for the little boys had to be got up to the top of the coach, and their boxes had to be brought out and put in. He was very busy seeing to all these arrangements, when his uncle, Mr Ralph Nickleby, accosted him.

"Oh! here you are, sir!" said Ralph. "And here are your mother and sister."

"Where?" said Nicholas, looking hastily round.

"Here!" replied his uncle. "Having too much money, and nothing at all to do with it, they were paying a hackney coach as I came up."

"We were afraid of being too late to see him before he went away from us," said Mrs Nickleby, embracing her son. "I should never have forgiven myself if I had not seen him. Poor dear boy—going away without his breakfast, too, because he feared to distress us!"

"Now, Nickleby," said Squeers, coming up, "I think you had better get up behind. I'm afraid of one of them boys falling off, and then there's twenty pound a year gone."

"Dear Nicholas," whispered Kate, touching her brother's arm, "who is that vulgar man?"

"Eh?" growled Ralph, whose quick ears had caught the whisper. "Do you wish to be introduced to Mr Squeers, my dear?"

"*That* the schoolmaster! No, uncle, oh, no!" replied Kate, shrinking back. And to Nicholas she whispered again, "Who is this man? What kind of a place can it be that you are going to?"

"I hardly know, Kate," replied Nicholas, pressing his sister's hand. "I suppose the Yorkshire folks are rather rough and uncultivated—that's all. Bless you, dear, and goodbye. Mother, look forward to our meeting again some day! Uncle, farewell! Thank you heartily for all you have done—and for all you mean to do—for my mother and sister." And, mounting nimbly to his seat, he waved his hand.

The porters were screwing the last reluctant sixpences

from the passengers, and the horses were impatiently rattling their harness, when Nicholas felt somebody pulling softly at his leg. He looked down, and there stood Newman Noggs, who pushed up into his hand a dirty letter.

"What's this?" inquired Nicholas.

"Hush!" rejoined Noggs, pointing to Ralph Nickleby, who was saying a few earnest words to Mr Squeers a short distance off. "Take it.—Read it.—Nobody knows.—That's all."

"Stop!" cried Nicholas. "Stop!" But Newman Noggs was gone.

A minute's bustle, a banging of the coach door, a swaying of the vehicle to one side, as the heavy coachman and still heavier guard climbed into their seats, a cry of "All right!" a few notes from the horn, and the coach was rattling over the stones of Smithfield.

The weather was bitterly cold; a great deal of snow fell from time to time; and the wind was intensely keen. Mr Squeers got down at almost every stage—to stretch his legs, as he said—and always came back with a very red nose. The little pupils ate the remains of their breakfast, went to sleep, woke, shivered, and cried. Nicholas tried to cheer the boys; and so the day wore on.

At Eton Slocomb there was a good hot dinner, of which all the grown-up passengers partook, while the five little boys were put to thaw by the fire, and regaled with sandwiches.

A stage or two further the lamps were lighted, and the night and the snow came on together.

There was no sound to be heard but the howling of the

wind; for the noise of the wheels and the tread of the horses' feet were rendered inaudible by the thick coating of snow which covered the ground.

Nicholas fell asleep towards morning. The day dragged on uncomfortably enough; and it was six o'clock that night before he and Mr Squeers and the five little boys were all put down at the George and New Inn, Greta Bridge.

Nicholas and the boys stood with their luggage in the road, amusing themselves by looking at the coach as it changed horses; and then there came out of the inn-yard a rusty pony-chaise and a cart, driven by two labouring men.

"Put the boys and the boxes into the cart," said Squeers; "but this young man and me will go in the chaise. Get in, Nickleby."

Nicholas obeyed. Mr Squeers induced the pony to obey also, and they started off, leaving the cart to follow.

"Is it much further to Dotheboys Hall, sir?" asked Nicholas.

"About three mile from here," replied Squeers. "But you needn't call it a Hall down here."

Nicholas coughed.

And Mr Squeers added, "The fact is, it ain't a Hall. We call it a Hall up in London because it sounds better. A man may call his house an island, if he likes. There's no Act of Parliament against that, I believe?"

"I believe not, sir" rejoined Nicholas, who had become very thoughtful.

Mr Squeers said nothing more, and lashed the pony

till they came to their journey's end. "Jump out," said
Squeers.— "Hallo there! Come and put this horse up.
Be quick, will you?"

Nicholas now saw that the school was a long, cold-
looking house, one storey high, with a few straggling
outbuildings behind, and a barn and stabling adjoining.
Then the noise of somebody unlocking the yard-gate
was heard, and presently a tall, lean boy with a lantern
in his hand issued forth.

"Is that you, Smike?" cried the schoolmaster.

"Yes, sir," replied the boy.

Mr Squeers got out of the chaise; and, after ordering
the boy to see to the pony, he told Nicholas to wait at the
front door a minute, while he went round and let him in.

4

Dotheboys Hall

A feeling of distrust and doubt seized Nicholas, and, looking up at the dreary house and dark windows, he felt a sinking of heart and spirit which he had never experienced before.

"Now, then, Nickleby!" cried Squeers, poking his head out at the front door. "The wind blows in at this door enough to knock a man off his legs. Come in."

Nicholas hurried in; and Mr Squeers ushered him into a small parlour scantily furnished with a few chairs and a couple of tables, one of which bore some preparations for supper.

They had not been in this apartment a couple of minutes when a woman bounced into the room, and, seizing Mr Squeers by the neck, gave him two loud kisses.

She was of a large, raw-boned figure, half a head taller than Mr Squeers, and was dressed in a dimity nightjacket, with her hair in papers. She had also a dirty nightcap on, relieved by a yellow cotton handkerchief, which tied it under the chin.

"How is my Squeery?" said this lady, in a playful manner, and a very hoarse voice.

"Quite well, my love," replied Squeers. "How's the cows?"

"All right, every one of 'em," answered the lady.

"Come, that's a blessing," said Squeers, pulling off his greatcoat. "The boys are all as they were, I suppose?"

"Oh, yes, *they're* well enough!" replied Mrs Squeers snappishly.

"This is the new young man, my dear," said Mr Squeers.

"Oh!" replied Mrs Squeers, nodding her head at Nicholas, and eyeing him coldly from top to toe.

"He'll take a meal with us tonight," said Mr Squeers, "and go among the boys tomorrow. You can give him a shake-down here tonight, can't you?"

"We must manage it somehow," replied the lady. "You don't much mind how you sleep, I suppose, sir?"

"No, indeed," said Nicholas. "I'm not particular."

"That's lucky," said Mrs Squeers. And then a young servant-girl brought in a Yorkshire pie and some cold beef, which being set upon the table, the boy Smike appeared with a jug of ale.

Mr Squeers was emptying his greatcoat pocket of letters to different pupils, and the boy glanced at them with an anxious and timid expression, as if with a hope that one among them might be for him.

Smike could not have been less than eighteen or nineteen years old, and was tall for that age; but he wore a suit such as is put upon very little boys, and which, though most absurdly short in the arms and legs, was quite wide enough for his thin and feeble frame.

On his feet were a very large pair of boots, that might have been worn by some stout farmer, but were now too patched and tattered for a beggar. Heaven knows how long he had been there, for round his neck was a tattered child's frill, only half concealed by a coarse man's neckerchief. He was lame; and as he pretended to be busy arranging the table, he glanced at the letters with a look so keen, and yet so hopeless, that Nicholas could hardly bear to watch him.

"What are you bothering about there, Smike?" cried Mrs Squeers.

"Oh! it's you, is it?" said Squeers, looking up.

"Yes, sir," replied the youth, pressing his hands together. "Is there—have you—did anybody—has anything been heard—about—me?"

"Not a word," replied Squeers testily.

The lad withdrew his eyes, and, putting his hand to his face, moved towards the door.

"Not a word," went on Squeers, "and never will be. Now this is a pretty sort of thing, isn't it, that you should have been left here all these years, and no money paid after the first six, nor no notice taken, nor no clue to be got who you belong to? It's a pretty sort of thing that I should have to feed a great fellow like you, and never hope to get one penny for it—isn't it?"

The boy put his hand to his head, and then, looking vacantly at his questioner, gradually broke into a smile and limped away.

"I'll tell you what, Squeers," remarked his wife, as the door closed; "I think that young chap's turning silly."

"I hope not," said the schoolmaster; "for he's a handy

fellow out of doors, and worth his meat and drink anyway. But come, let's have supper, for I am hungry and tired, and want to get to bed."

Then a hot steak was brought in especially for Mr Squeers, and he and Nicholas drew up their chairs.

"What'll the young man take, my dear?" asked Mrs Squeers.

"Whatever he likes that's present," answered Squeers.

"What do you say, Mr Knuckleboy?" inquired Mrs Squeers.

"I'll take a little of the pie, if you please," said Nicholas. "A very little, for I'm not hungry;" for he felt that his appetite was quite taken away.

"Well, it's a pity to cut the pie if you're not hungry, isn't it?" said Mrs Squeers. "Will you try a bit of the beef?"

"Whatever you please," replied Nicholas, in an absent manner. "It's all the same to me."

Mrs Squeers looked vastly gracious on receiving this reply, and—nodding to Mr Squeers as much as to say that she was glad to find the young man knew his station—helped Nicholas to a slice of meat, with her own fair hands.

Supper being over, and removed by the small servant-girl with a hungry eye, Mrs Squeers retired to lock it up, and also to take into custody the clothes of the five boys that had just arrived.

The new pupils were regaled with a light supper of porridge, and stowed away, side by side, in a small bedstead, to warm each other, and to dream of a substantial meal with something hot after it.

After that Mr Squeers yawned fearfully, and Mrs

Squeers and the girl dragged in a small mattress and a couple of blankets, and arranged them into a bed for Nicholas.

"We'll put you into your regular bedroom tomorrow, Nickleby," said Squeers. "Let me see! Who sleeps in Brooks's bed, my dear?"

"In Brooks's?" said Mrs Squeers, pondering "There's Jennings, little Bolder, Graymarsh, and What's-his-name."

"So there is," rejoined Squeers. "Yes. Brooks is full."

"Full!" thought Nicholas. "I should think he was."

"There's a place somewhere, I know," said Squeers. "However, we'll have that all settled tomorrow. Goodnight, Nickleby. Seven o'clock in the morning, mind."

"I shall be ready, sir," replied Nicholas. "Goodnight."

"I'll come in myself and show you where the well is," said Squeers. "You'll always find a little bit of soap in the kitchen window. That belongs to you. I don't know, I'm sure," added Squeers, "whose towel to put you on; but if you'll make shift with something tomorrow morning, Mrs Squeers will arrange that in the course of the day."

"And mind you take care, young man, and get first wash," put in Mrs Squeers. "The teacher ought always to have it; but the boys get the better of him, if they can."

They then retired, leaving Nicholas alone, and he took half-a-dozen turns up and down the room in a state of much agitation and excitement. But growing gradually calmer, he sat himself down in a chair, and resolved that, come what might, he would endeavour, for a time, to bear whatever wretchedness might be in store for him; and that, remembering the helplessness of his mother and sister, he would give his uncle no excuse for deserting them in their need.

After that he grew less desponding, and even hoped that affairs at Dotheboys Hall might yet prove better than they promised.

He was preparing for bed, when a sealed letter fell from his coat pocket. In the hurry of leaving London it had escaped his attention, but it at once brought back to him the recollection of the mysterious behaviour of Newman Noggs. It was directed to himself, and he read as follows:—

MY DEAR YOUNG MAN,—I know the world. You do not, or you would not be bound on such a journey. If ever you should want to shelter in London (don't be angry at this, I once thought I never should), they will tell you where I live at the sign of the Crown, in Silver Street, Golden Square. You can come at night. Once nobody was ashamed —never mind that. It's all over. I was a gentleman once—I was indeed. 'Excuse errors. I should forget how to wear a whole coat now. I have forgotten all my old ways. My spelling may have gone with them.

NEWMAN NOGGS

As Nicholas folded this letter and placed it in his pocket-book, his eyes were dimmed with tears.

He slept sound on his hard bed, for he was tired after his long, cold drive; and he dreamed that he was making his fortune very fast indeed, when the faint glimmer of a candle shone before his eyes, and the voice of Mr Squeers aroused him.

"Past seven, Nickleby," said the schoolmaster.

"Has morning come already?" said Nicholas, sitting up in bed.

"Ah! that it has," replied Squeers; "and ready iced, too. Now, Nickleby, come; tumble up."

Nickleby 'tumbled up' at once, and began to dress himself by the light of the taper that Mr Squeers carried.

"Here's a pretty go," said that gentleman; "the pump's froze. You can't wash yourself this morning."

"Not wash myself!" exclaimed Nicholas.

"No, not a bit of it," rejoined Squeers tartly. "So you must be content with giving yourself a dry polish till we break the ice in the well, and can get a bucketful out for the boys. Don't stand staring at me, but do look sharp—will you?"

Nicholas huddled on his clothes, while Squeers opened the shutters and blew the candle out; when the voice of Mrs Squeers was heard outside demanding admittance.

"Come in, my love," said Squeers.

Mrs Squeers came in, still dressed in the nightjacket. She also wore an old beaver bonnet, stuck with much ease and lightness on the top of her nightcap. "Drat the things!" said the lady, opening the cupboard. "I can't find the school spoon anywhere. And it's brimstone morning."

"We purify the boys' bloods now and then, Nickleby," said Mr Squeers.

"Purify fiddlesticks' ends," said the lady. "Don't think, young man, that we go to the expense of flower of brimstone and molasses just to purify them; because if you think we carry out the business in that way, you'll find yourself mistaken; and so I tell you plainly."

"My dear!" said Mr Squeers, frowning. "Hem!"

"Oh! nonsense. If the young man comes to be a teacher here, let him understand, at once, that we don't want any foolery about the boys. They have the brimstone and treacle, partly because, if they hadn't something or other in the way of medicine, they'd be always ailing and giving a world of trouble; and partly because it spoils their appetites, and comes cheaper than breakfast and dinner." And having found the spoon, the lady hurried away.

"A most invaluable woman that, Nickleby," said Squeers. "I don't know her equal. She's a mother to them boys. She does things for them boys, Nickleby, that I don't believe half the mothers going would do for their own sons."

"I should think they would not, sir," returned Nicholas.

"Come," said Squeers, "let's go to the schoolroom. And lend me a hand with my school coat—will you?"

Nicholas assisted his master to put on an old, fustian shooting-jacket, which he took down from a peg in the passage. And Squeers, arming himself with his cane, led the way across a yard to a door at the back of the house.

"There," said the schoolmaster, as they stepped in together; "this is our shop, Nickleby."

It was such a crowded scene, that at first Nicholas

stared about him, really without seeing anything at all. Then he found that he was in a bare and dirty room, having a couple of windows with many broken panes of glass stopped up with old copybooks and paper.

There were a couple of long, old rickety desks, cut and notched, and inked and broken here and there; two or three forms; a separate desk for Squeers; and another for his assistant.

But the pupils! Nicholas looked at them in dismay. Pale and haggard faces, lank and bony figures, boys of stunted growth, and others whose long, meagre legs could hardly bear their stooping bodies.

There were boys with sore eyes, boys with harelips, boys with crooked feet; children whose parents had never loved them; others whose parents were dead. There were little faces that should have been handsome, darkened with the scowl of sullen, dogged suffering.

Mrs Squeers stood at one of the desks, presiding over an immense basin of brimstone and treacle, of which mixture she thrust into each boy's mouth in succession a large, wooden spoonful.

In another corner, huddled together for companionship, were the five little boys who had arrived the night before, three of them in very large leather breeches, and two in old trousers, a something tighter fit than drawers are usually worn.

At no great distance from these was seated the young son and heir of Mr Squeers—a striking likeness of his father—kicking hard, while Smike was fitting on him a pair of new boots that bore a most suspicious resemblance to those which one of the new pupils had worn on the journey from London.

"Now," said Mr Squeers, giving the desk a great rap with his cane, which made half the boys nearly jump out of their boots, "is that physicking over?"

"Just over," said Mrs Squeers, choking the last boy in her hurry, and tapping the crown of his head with the wooden spoon to restore him. "Here, you, Smike! Take away now. Look sharp!"

Smike shuffled out with the basin, and Mrs Squeers, having called up a little boy with a curly head, and wiped her hands upon it, hurried out after Smike into a kind of wash-house, where there was a small fire, and a large kettle—together with a number of little wooden bowls which were arranged on a board.

Into these bowls, assisted by the hungry servant, Mrs Squeers poured a portion of porridge. A small piece of bread was placed in each bowl, and, when they had eaten their porridge, with the help of the bread, the boys ate the bread itself, and breakfast was finished. Then Mr Squeers said in a solemn voice, "For what we have received may the Lord make us truly thankful!"—and went away to his own.

Nicholas also had a bowl of porridge, which he swallowed because there was nothing else to eat. And—being the assistant master—he was afterwards allowed a slice of bread and butter. Then, having nothing else to do, Nicholas sat himself down to wait for school-time.

He could not but see how silent and sad the boys all seemed to be. There was none of the noise and clamour of a schoolroom; none of its boisterous play and mirth. The children sat crouching and shivering together, and seemed to have no spirit to move about.

The only pupil that showed the slightest sign of play-fulness was Master Squeers, and—as his chief amuse-ment was to tread upon the other boys' toes in his new boots—his playfulness was rather disagreeable.

After some half-hour's delay, Mr Squeers reappeared; the boys took their places and their books, and the mas-ter called up the first class. They stood in a row in front of the master's desk—half-a-dozen of them, out at knees and elbows—one of them placing a torn and dirty book beneath his eye.

"This is the first class in English spelling, Nickleby," said Mr Squeers, beckoning Nicholas to stand beside him. "We'll get up a Latin one and hand that over to you. Now, then, where's the first boy?"

"Please, sir, he's cleaning the back-parlour window," said the present head of the spelling class.

"So he is, to be sure," rejoined Squeers. "We go upon the practical mode of teaching, Nickleby—the regular education system. C-l-e-a-n, clean, verb active, to make bright, to scour. W-i-n, win, d-e-r, winder, a casement. When the boy knows this out of book, he goes and does it. Where's the second boy?"

"Please, sir, he's weeding the garden," replied a small voice.

"To be sure," said Squeers. "So he is. B-o-t, bot, t-i-n, tin, bottin, n-e-y, bottinney, noun substantive, a knowl-edge of plants. When he knows that bottinney means a knowledge of plants, he goes and knows 'em. That's our system, Nickleby. What do you think of it?"

"It is a very useful one, at any rate," answered Nicholas.

"I believe you," rejoined Squeers "Third boy, what's a horse?"

"A beast, sir," replied the boy.

"So it is," said Squeers. "Ain't it, Nickleby?"

"I believe there is no doubt of that, sir," answered Nicholas.

"Of course there isn't," answered Squeers. "A horse is a quadruped, and quadruped's Latin for beast, as everybody that's gone through the grammar knows, or else where's the use of having grammars at all? As you're perfect in that," went on Squeers, turning to the boy, "go and look after my horse, and rub him down well, or I'll rub you down. The rest of the class go and draw water up till somebody tells you to leave off, for it's washing day tomorrow, and they want the coppers filled.'

So saying, he dismissed the first class, and eyed Nicholas with a look half cunning, and half doubtful.

"That's the way we do it, Nickleby," he said, after a pause.

Nicholas shrugged his shoulders, and said he saw it was.

"And a very good way it is," said Mr Squeers. Now, just take them fourteen little boys, and hear them some reading, because you know you must begin to be useful."

The children were then arranged in a half circle round the new master, and he was soon listening to their dull, drawling, hesitating voices. In this manner the morning lagged wearily on.

At one o'clock the boys, having first had their appetites taken away by stir-about and potatoes, sat down in the kitchen to some hard salt beef. After this there was another hour of crouching in the schoolroom and shivering with cold, and then school began again.

It was Mr Squeers's custom to call the boys together, and make a sort of report, after every half-yearly visit to London, regarding the relations and friends he had seen, the letters he had brought down, the bills which had been paid, and the bills which had been left unpaid.

The boys were recalled from window, garden, stable, and cow-yard, and the whole school was gathered together, when Mr Squeers, with a small bundle of papers in his hand, and Mrs Squeers, following with a pair of canes, entered the room.

"Boys, I've been to London," said Mr Squeers, "and have returned to my family and you, as strong and well as ever. I have seen the parents of some boys, and they're so glad to hear how their sons are getting on, that there's no prospect of their going away. Bolder's father was two pound ten short. Where is Bolder?"

An unhealthy-looking boy stepped to the master's desk, and raised his eyes imploringly to the master's face.

"Bolder!" said Squeers, "if your father thinks that because—" he paused. "Bolder, you are a rascal!"—and shutting his ears to a piteous cry for mercy, Squeers fell upon the boy, and caned him soundly. "Oh! you won't hold that noise, won't you? Put him out, Smike."

Smike bundled the wretched Bolder out by a side door, and Mr Squeers perched himself again on his own stool. "Now let us see," said Squeers. "A letter for Cobbey. Stand up, Cobbey."

Another boy stood up, and eyed the letter very hard.

"Oh!" said Squeers: "Cobbey's grandmother is dead, which is all the news his sister sends, except eighteen-pence, which will just pay for that broken square of glass. Mrs Squeers, my dear, will you take the money?"

Mrs Squeers pocketed the eighteen-pence with the most business-like air. And Squeers passed to the next boy.

"Stand up, Graymarsh."

Another boy stood up, and the schoolmaster looked over the letter, as before.

"Graymarsh's aunt is very glad to hear he's so well and happy, and sends her respectful compliments to Mrs Squeers, and thinks she must be an angel. She likewise thinks Mr Squeers is too good for this world. She hopes Graymarsh will love Master Squeers, and not object to sleeping five in a bed, which no Christian should. "Ah!" said Squeers, folding it up, "a delightful letter!"

Then Graymarsh sat down, and Mr Squeers having called out "Mobbs!" another boy rose.

"Mobbs's stepmother took to her bed on hearing that he wouldn't eat fat," went on Mr Squeers, "and has been ill ever since. She is sorry to find he is discontented, and has given his double-bladed knife, with a corkscrew in it, to the missionaries. Mobbs, come to me."

Mobbs moved slowly towards the desk, rubbing his eyes; and soon after he, too, retired by the side door, weeping bitterly.

Mr Squeers then proceeded to open many other letters; some enclosing money, which Mrs Squeers 'took care of.'

This business finished, a few slovenly lessons were

performed, and Mr Squeers retired to his own fireside, leaving Nicholas to take care of the boys in the schoolroom, which was very cold, and where a meal of bread and cheese was served out shortly after dark.

There was a small stove at that corner of the room which was nearest to the master's desk, and by it Nicholas sat down, feeling greatly depressed, and utterly miserable.

The cruelty of which he had been an unwilling witness, the coarse and ruffianly behaviour of Squeers, the dirty room, the sights and sounds of weeping, filled him with honest disgust and indignation; and he felt for the moment as though he could never lift up his head again.

But for the present his resolve was taken. He must not think of leaving this dreadful place yet awhile, for his mother and sister depended too much on his uncle's favour, and he dared not risk awakening Ralph Nickleby's anger by giving up his post just then.

Full of these thoughts, Nicholas all at once encountered the upturned face of Smike, who was on his knees before the stove, picking a few stray cinders from the hearth, and placing them on the fire. The lad had paused to steal a look at Nicholas, and when he saw that he was observed, he shrank back, as if expecting a blow.

"You need not fear me," said Nicholas "Are you cold?"

"N-no."

"You are shivering."

"I am not cold," said Smike quickly. "I am used to it."

He looked so much afraid of giving offence, and he was such a timid, broken-spirited creature, that

Nicholas could not help exclaiming, "Poor fellow!"

If he had struck Smike, the poor lad would have slunk away without a word. But now he burst into tears. "Oh, dear—oh, dear!" he cried, covering his face with his cracked and horny hands "My heart will break. It will—it will!"

"Hush!" said Nicholas, laying his hand upon his shoulder. "Be a man. You are nearly one by years. God help you."

"By years!" cried Smike. "Oh, dear, dear—how many of them! How many of them since I was a little child, younger than any that are here now. Where are they all?"

"Whom do you speak of?" said Nicholas. "Tell me."

"My friends," he replied, "myself—my—oh! what sufferings have been mine. Do you remember the boy that died here?"

"I was not here, you know," said Nicholas gently. "But what of him?"

"Why," replied the youth, drawing nearer to Nicholas's side, "I was with him at night, and when it was all silent, he cried no more for friends he wished to come and sit with him, but began to see faces round his bed—faces that came from home. And he said they smiled, and he died, lifting his face to kiss them. Do you hear?"

"Yes, yes," said Nicholas.

"What faces will smile on me when I die?" cried the poor fellow, shivering. "they would frighten me, for I should not know them. No hope—no hope!"

The bell rang to bed. And the boy, falling at the sound into his usual listless state, crept away, as if anxious to avoid notice.

And with a heavy heart, Nicholas followed to his dirty and crowded dormitory.

5

Miss Squeers's Tea-Party

When Mr Squeers left the schoolroom for his own fireside, he retired to a small apartment at the back of the house, where sat Mrs Squeers, their daughter Miss Fanny Squeers, and their son Master Wackford Squeers.

Miss Squeers, who was twenty-two years of age, had been spending a few days with a neighbouring friend, and had only just returned home.

"Well, my dear," said Mr Squeers, drawing up his chair, "what do you think of the new teacher?"

"Oh! that Knuckleboy," said Mrs Squeers impatiently. "I hate him. He is a proud, haughty, consequential, turned-up-nosed peacock."

"Hem!" said Mr Squeers. "He is cheap, my dear. The young man is very cheap. Five pound a year."

"It's dear, if you don't want him—isn't it?" replied his wife.

"But we do want him," urged Squeers.

"Don't tell me," retorted Mrs Squeers. "You can put in the advertisements, 'Education by Mr Wackford Squeers and able assistants,' without having any assistants—can't you?"

"In this matter of having a teacher," said Mr Squeers sternly, "I'll take my own way; and I'll have a man under me till such time as little Wackford is able to take charge of the school."

"Am I to take care of the school when I grow up a man, father?" said little Wackford.

"You are, my son," returned Mr Squeers.

"Oh, my eye—won't I give it to the boys!" exclaimed Wackford, grasping his father's cane. "Oh, father, won't I make 'em squeak again!"

Mr and Mrs Squeers both gave a shout of laughter, and Mr Squeers pressed a penny into his son's hand.

"He's a nasty, stuck-up monkey, that Knuckleboy," went on Mrs Squeers. "It shall be no fault of mine if I don't bring his pride down. I watched him when you were laying on to little Bolder this afternoon. He looked as black as thunder all the while, and one time started up, as if he had more than got into his head to make a rush at you."

"Who is the man, father?" asked Miss Squeers, with great curiosity.

"Why, your father has got some nonsense in his head, that he's the son of a poor gentleman that died the other day."

This made Miss Fanny Squeers more and more curious about the new master; and when she retired for the night, she questioned the hungry servant very closely regarding the outward appearance of Nicholas.

The girl returned such enthusiastic remarks about his beautiful dark eyes, his sweet smile, and his straight legs, that Miss Squeers made up her mind that she would have to look at Nicholas herself the very next day.

So, watching the opportunity of her mother being engaged, and her father absent, she went into the schoolroom to get a pen mended, where, seeing nobody but Nicholas looking after the boys, she blushed very deeply, and showed great confusion.

"I beg your pardon," faltered Miss Squeers. I thought my father was—Dear me, How very awkward!"

"Mr Squeers is out," said Nicholas

"I never knew anything happen so cross," exclaimed the young lady, blushing once more, and glancing from the pen in her hand to Nicholas at his desk, and back again.

"If that is all you want," said Nicholas, smiling and pointing to the pen, "perhaps I can supply his place."

"He *has* a beautiful smile," thought Miss Squeers; and she put the pen into the new master's hand, with a most winning manner.

Nicholas made the pen; but when he gave it to Miss Squeers, Miss Squeers dropped it; and when he stooped to pick it up, Miss Squeers stooped also, and they knocked their heads together—at which five and twenty little boys laughed aloud; being positively for first and only time that half year.

"Very awkward of me," said Nicholas, opening the door.

"Not at all, sir," replied Miss Squeers. "It was my fault." And as she walked away, she added to herself, "I never saw such straight legs in the whole course of my life."

In fact, Miss Squeers was in love with Nicholas Nickleby.

Now the friend with whom Miss Squeers had been to stay with was 'Tilda Price, the miller's daughter, who had just become engaged to be married to John Browdie, the corn factor.

'Tilda Price was eighteen years old, and Miss Squeers—rather vexed that her friend, four years younger than herself, was already engaged to be married—put on her bonnet with great haste, and made her way to Miss Price's house; and, with an air of great secrecy, whispered—that she was not exactly engaged, but was going to be to a gentleman's son, who had come to Dotheboys Hall, under most mysterious circumstances.

"But what has he said to you?" asked 'Tilda Price.

"Don't ask me what he said, my dear," rejoined Miss Squeers. "If you had only seen his looks and smiles! I never was so overcome in all my life"

"How I should like to see him!" exclaimed her friend.

"So you shall, 'Tilda," replied Miss Squeers. "I think Mother's going away for two days to fetch some boys; and, when she does, I'll ask you and John up to tea, and have him to meet you."

It so fell out that Mrs Squeers's journey was fixed for the next day but one, and as Mr Squeers was going to drive over to the market town that same afternoon, he gave his daughter his consent for her to invite her friends, and told Nicholas that he was expected to take tea in the parlour that evening at five o'clock.

"Where's John, 'Tilda?" said Miss Squeers, when Miss Price arrived.

"Only gone home to clean himself," replied her friend. "He will be here by the time the tea's drawn."

Then somebody tapped at the parlour door. "Come in," cried Miss Squeers faintly. And in walked Nicholas.

"Good evening," he said. "I understand from Mr Squeers that—"

"Oh, yes, it's all right!" interrupted Miss Squeers. "Father don't tea with us, but you won't mind that, I dare say. We are only waiting for one more gentleman."

In a few minutes the corn factor turned up, with his hair very damp from recent washing, and a clean shirt, with a very large collar, and a white waistcoat.

"Mr Nickleby—Mr John Browdie," said Miss Squeers.

"Servant, sir," said John, who was something over six feet high, with a face and body in due proportion.

"Yours to command, sir," replied Nicholas.

Then they sat down to tea, and it was a sight to see how he and Nicholas emptied the plate of bread-and-butter between them.

"Ye wean't get bread-and-butther every night, mun," said Mr Browdie, after he had sat staring at Nicholas a long time over the empty plate

Nicholas bit his lip and coloured.

"Ecod!" said Mr Browdie, "ye'll be nowt but skeen and boans if you stop here long eneaf. Ho! ho! ho! T'other teacher, 'cod he wur a lean 'un, he wur."

"Your remarks are offensire, Mr Browdie," said Nicholas

"If you say another word, John," cried Miss Price, "I'll never speak to you again."

"Come," said Miss Squeers, leaving the table, "we're going to have a game of cards."

And the hearth being swept up, and the candle snuffed, they sat down to play Speculation.

"There are only four of us, 'Tilda," said Miss Squeers, looking slily at Nicholas. "So we had better go partners, two against two."

"What do you say, Mr Nickleby?" inquired Miss Price, who was very pretty and rather coquettish

"With all the pleasure in life," replied Nicholas. And so saying—quite unconscious of giving offence— he gathered, into one common heap, the counters allotted to Miss Price and to himself.

"Mr Browdie," said Miss Squeers hysterically—for she had intended to play with Nicholas herself— "shall we make a bank against them?"

The big Yorkshireman seemed quite overwhelmed by the new teacher's impudence in taking for his partner the girl to whom he was himself engaged, and consented gruffly; while 'Tilda Price giggled

The deal fell to Nicholas, and the hand prospered. "We intend to win everything," he said.

"Tilda has won something she didn't expect, I think," said Miss Squeers maliciously; while the Yorkshireman flattened his nose once or twice with his clenched fist.

"I never had much luck, really!" exclaimed the mischievous Miss Price, after another hand or two. "It's all along of you, Mr Nickleby, I think. I should like to have you for a partner always."

"I wish you had," said Nicholas.

It was a sight to see how Miss Squeers tossed her head, and the corn factor flattened his nose, let alone Miss Price's joy in making them jealous, and Nicholas's happy unconsciousness that he was making anybody uncomfortable.

"We have all the talking to ourselves," he said, looking good-humouredly round the table, as he took up the cards for a fresh deal.

"You do it so well," tittered Miss Squeers, "that it would be a pity to interrupt—wouldn't it, Mr Browdie?"

"We'll talk to you, you know, if you'll say anything," said the teasing Miss Price "John, why don't you say something?"

"Say summat?" repeated the big Yorkshireman, striking the table heavily with his fist. "Dang my boans and boddy, if I stan' this ony longer. Do ye gang whoam wi' me, and let yon young whipster look sharp out for a broken head next time he comes under my hond."

"Mercy on us, what's all this?" cried Miss Price, looking very much surprised.

"Come whoam, tell'ee, come whoam," replied the Yorkshireman sternly, while Miss Squeers burst into a shower of tears.

"Why, and here's Fanny in tears now!" exclaimed Miss Price, more and more surprised. "What *can* be the matter?"

"Oh! you don't know, miss, of course you don't know," sobbed Miss Squeers. "Pray don't trouble yourself to inquire. I hate you, 'Tilda"

"You are very polite, ma'am," returned Miss Price, curtseying very low. "Wish you a very good night, ma'am, and pleasant dreams attend your sleep." With that, Miss Price swept from the room, followed by John Browdie, who cast at Nicholas an angry scowl.

Miss Squeers cried harder than ever, and Nicholas, after looking on for a few seconds, walked off very quietly, while Miss Squeers was moaning in her pocket-handkerchief.

"I have set these people by the ears, it seems," muttered Nicholas; "and I have made two new enemies, where, Heaven knows, I needed none." So saying, he felt his way among the throng of weary-hearted sleepers, and crept into his poor bed.

The day after, there came a knock at the front door, and the hungry servant showed in Miss Price.

"Well, Fanny," said the miller's daughter, "you see I have come to see you, although we had some words last night."

"I bear no malice, 'Tilda," replied Miss Squeers. "I am above it."

"But come now, Fanny," said Miss Price, "I want to have a word with you about young Mr Nickleby."

"He is nothing to me," interrupted Miss Squeers. "I despise him too much. Oh! 'Tilda! how could you have acted so mean and dishonourable?"

"Heyday!" exclaimed Miss Price, giggling. "All this because I happen to have enough good looks to make people civil to me. Persons don't make their own faces!"

"Hold your tongue, 'Tilda," began Miss Squeers in a very shrill voice; and she was just on the verge of tears, when Miss Price embraced and soothed her, and then suggested that Fanny should walk with her part of the way home. Miss Squeers agreeing, the girls started off, and soon came within sight of Nicholas, who happened to be taking a melancholy stroll.

"I feel fit to drop into the earth, 'Tilda," gasped Miss Squeers.

Nicholas, walking with his eyes upon the ground, was not aware of their approach until they were close upon him. "Good morning," he said, bowing and passing by.

"He is going," murmured Miss Squeers. "I shall choke, 'Tilda."

"Come back, Mr Nickleby, do!" cried Miss Price. "Come back! Fanny was too hasty with you yesterday, Mr Nickleby."

Mr Nickleby came back, and looked very much confused, at which Miss Price's eyes danced with merriment.

"Haven't you got anything to say?" said the mischievous girl.

"I am very sorry," hesitated Nicholas— "truly sorry —for having been the cause of any difference among you last night."

"Well; that's not all you have to say, surely?" exclaimed Miss Price.

"I fear there is something more," stammered Nicholas, looking towards the blushing Miss Squeers. "It is a most awkward thing to say—but may I ask if that young lady supposes I am in love with her?"

"Of course she does," rejoined Miss Price.

"She does!" almost shouted Nicholas.

"If Mr Nickleby has doubted that, 'Tilda," said Miss Squeers, blushing more and more, "he may set his mind at rest. His love is returned"

"Stop!" cried Nicholas hurriedly. "Pray hear me. This is the greatest mistake that ever human being laboured under. I have scarcely seen the young lady half-a-dozen times, but if I had seen her sixty times it would be precisely the same." And with this particularly straightforward declaration, and very indignant, and greatly excited, Nicholas retreated as fast as he could.

But poor Miss Squeers! Refused! Refused by a teacher, picked up by advertisement, at a yearly salary of £5! And this, too, in the presence of a little chit of a miller's daughter of eighteen! She could have choked in right good earnest. And from that moment she detested Nicholas with all her might.

Indeed, he had not a friend among the Squeers family; and when they discovered that the poor drudge Smike had become his devoted slave, they hated Nicholas more and more. For Smike, since the night Nicholas had spoken to him kindly, had followed him to and fro, with a restless desire to serve or help him.

He would sit beside Nicholas for hours, looking patiently at him; and a word would brighten up his careworn face, and call into it a passing gleam of even happiness. Smike was an altered being. He had an object now; and that object was to show his attachment to the only person who had treated him like a human creature.

Squeers was jealous of the influence that the new teacher had so quickly acquired; and it was no sooner observed that Smike had become attached to Nicholas, than stripes and blows, morning, noon, and night were the poor lad's only portion.

Nicholas had arranged a few regular lessons for the boys; and one night as he paced up and down the dismal schoolroom, his heart almost bursting to think that his protection should have increased the misery of the wretched Smike, he paused in a dark corner where sat the object of his thoughts.

Poor Smike was poring over a tattered book, vainly trying to master some lesson which a child of nine years old could conquer with ease, but which, to the puzzled brain of the crushed boy of nineteen, was an impossible task. Yet there he sat, patiently studying the page, inspired by the one desire to please his only friend.

Nicholas laid his hand upon his shoulder.

"I can't do it," said the dejected creature, looking up with bitter disappointment. "No, no," and closing the book with a sigh, Smike laid his head upon his arm. He was weeping.

"Do not, for Heaven's sake!" said Nicholas in an agitated voice. "I cannot bear to see you."

"They are more hard with me than ever," sobbed the boy.

"I know it," rejoined Nicholas. "They are."

"But for you," said the poor lad, "I should die. They would kill me. They would. I know they would."

"You will do better, poor fellow," replied Nicholas mournfully, "when I am gone."

"Gone!" cried Smike, looking earnestly into his face. "are you going?"

"I cannot say," replied Nicholas.

"Tell me," said the boy imploringly, "oh! do tell me— *will* you go—*will* you?"

"I shall be driven to that at last!" said Nicholas. "The world is before me, after all."

"Tell me," urged Smike, "is the world as bad and dismal a place as this?"

"Heaven forbid!" returned Nicholas. "Its hardest, coarsest toil were happiness to this."

"Should I ever meet you there?" demanded the boy, speaking with unusual wildness.

"Yes," replied Nicholas, willing to soothe him.

"No, no!" said Smike, clasping him by the hand. "Should I—should I? Tell me that again. Say I should be sure to find you."

"You would," replied Nicholas, still trying to soothe him. "And I would help and aid you, and not bring fresh sorrow on you, as I have done here."

The boy caught both the young man's hands in his, and, hugging them to his breast, uttered a few broken words which Nicholas could not catch. Squeers entered at that moment, and Smike shrank back into his old corner.

Having provided for his nephew so successfully, Mr Ralph Nickleby next proceeded to procure some employment for his niece Kate; and succeeded in getting her a situation at the establishment of a very fashionable West-end milliner and dressmaker, named Madame Mantalini, who—very much taken with Kate's refined appearance and graceful figure—engaged her to try on mantles and jackets in the showroom for the customers.

A liveried footman showed Kate and Ralph Nickleby out of Madame Mantalini's private door; and Kate began to thank her uncle gratefully, when Ralph stopped her.

"Your mother has a little money?" he said.

"A very little," replied Kate.

"A little will go a long way, if it's used sparingly,"

said Ralph. "there is a house empty that belongs to me. I can put you into it until it is let, where you can both live rent free."

"Is it far from here, sir?" inquired Kate.

"Pretty well," said Ralph. "It's at the East-end. But I'll send my clerk down to you, at five o'clock on Saturday, to take you there. Goodbye. You know your way? Straight on."

Coldly shaking his niece's hand, Ralph left her at the top of Regent Street, and Kate walked sadly back to their lodgings in the Strand.

Saturday afternoon soon came, and punctual to his time, Newman Noggs limped up to the door, and knocked exactly as the church clocks were striking five.

"From Mr Ralph Nickleby," he said, when he got up-stairs.

"We shall be ready directly," said Kate

Then the coach which Newman had ordered came up, and they bade a sorrowful goodbye to the good-hearted Miss La Crevy.

They drove into the City, turning down by the river-side, and stopped in front of a large old dingy house in Thames Street.

Newman opened the door with a key which he took out of his hat, and led the way inside. Old, and gloomy, and dark it was, with an empty dog kennel; and pieces of old casks lay strewn about.

"This house depresses and chills one," said Kate. "How frowning and dark it looks!"

Newman appeared not to hear these remarks, but led the ladies to a couple of rooms on the first floor. In one were a few chairs, a table, and an old hearth rug; and a fire was ready laid in the grate. In the other stood an old tent-bedstead, and a few scant articles of bedroom furniture.

"Now, isn't this considerate of your uncle?" said Mrs Nickleby, trying to be pleased. "Why, we should not have had anything but the bed we bought yesterday to lie down upon, if it hadn't been for his thoughtfulness."

Newman Noggs did not say that *he* had hunted up the old furniture they saw; or that he had taken in the halfpenny-worth of milk for tea that stood upon a shelf, or filled the rusty kettle on the hob, or collected the woodchips from the wharf, or begged the coal.

But the idea of Ralph Nickleby having directed it to be done, tickled Newman so much, that he cracked all his ten fingers in succession.

"We need detain you no longer, I think," said Kate.

"Is there nothing I can do?" asked Newman.

"Nothing, thank you," rejoined Kate.

"Perhaps, my dear, Mr Noggs would like to drink our healths," said Mrs Nickleby, fumbling in her purse for a small tip.

"I think, Mamma," said Kate, hesitating, and remarking how Newman turned his face away, "I think you would hurt his feelings if you offered it."

Newman Noggs bowed to the young lady, more like a gentleman than the miserable creature he looked, and—pausing for a moment with the air of man who struggles to speak, but is uncertain what to say—quitted the room. Then the heavy door closed on its latch, and the ladies were left alone their dreary home.

6

The Runaway

The cold, feeble dawn of a January morning was stealing in at the windows of the boys' sleeping-room, when the voice of Mr Squeers was heard calling from the bottom of the stairs.

"Now then," cried Squeers, "are you going to sleep all day up there?"

"We shall be down directly, sir," replied Nicholas.

"Ah! you had better be down directly," answered Squeers, "or I'll be down on some of you. Where's that Smike?"

Nicholas looked hurriedly round the room, but made no answer.

"Smike!" shouted Squeers.

"Do you want your head broke in a fresh place, Smike?" demanded Mrs Squeers.

Still there was no reply, and still Nicholas stared about him, as did the greater part of the boys.

"Nickleby!" shouted Squeers, rapping the stair-rail impatiently with his cane.

"Well, sir?"

"Send that obstinate scoundrel down. Don't you hear me calling?"

"He is not here, sir," replied Nicholas.

"Don't tell me a lie," retorted the schoolmaster. "He is."

"He is not," answered Nicholas angrily. "Don't tell me one."

"We shall soon see that," said Squeers, rushing upstairs. "I'll find him, I warrant you." And Mr Squeers bounced into the dormitory, and swinging his cane, darted into the corner where the lean body of Smike was usually stretched at night. The cane descended harmlessly on the ground. There was nobody there.

"What does this mean?" said Squeers, turning round with a very pale face. "Where have you hid him?"

"I have seen nothing of him since last night," said Nicholas

"Come," said Squeers, evidently frightened,— "where is he?"

"Please, sir," said a small shrill voice, "I think Smike's run away, sir."

"You think he has run away, do you, sir?" demanded Squeers. "And what, sir," he added, catching the little boy who had spoken suddenly by the arms, "what reason have you to suppose that any boy should want to run away from this establishment?— Eh, sir?"

The child raised a dismal cry, and Mr Squeers, raising his cane, beat him until the little boy, in his writhings, actually rolled out of his hands.

"There!" said Squeers. "Now, if any other boy thinks that Smike has run away, I shall be glad to have a talk with him. Well, Nickleby! You think he has run away, I suppose?"

"I think it extremely likely," replied Nicholas

"Oh! you do, do you?" sneered Squeers.

Mrs Squeers had listened to this conversation from the bottom of the stairs; but now, losing all patience, she hastily made her way to the scene of action.

"What's all this here to-do?" said Mrs Squeers, as the boys fell off right and left, to save her clearing a passage with her brawny arms.

"Why, my dear," said Squeers, "the fact is that Smike is not to be found."

"And where's the wonder?" retorted Mrs Squeers. "If you get a parcel of proud-stomached teachers, that set the young dogs a-rebelling—what else can you look for? Now, young man, you just take yourself off to the schoolroom, and take the boys with you. I wouldn't keep such as you in the house another hour, if I had my way."

"Nor would you, if I had mine," retorted Nicholas. "Now, boys!"

"Ah! Now, boys!" mimicked Mrs Squeers. "Follow your leader, boys; and take pattern by Smike, if you dare. Come! Away with you!" With these words, she dismissed the boys; and had no sooner succeeded in clearing the room than she confronted her husband alone. "He is off," whispered Mrs Squeers. "He's not downstairs, for the girl has looked. He must have gone York way, and by a public road, too."

"Why must he?" inquired Squeers.

"Stupid!" answered Mrs Squeers. "He hadn't any money—had he? So he must beg his way, and he could do that nowhere but on the public road."

"That's true," exclaimed Squeers.

"Now, if you take the chaise, and go one road," said his wife, "and I borrow Swallow's chaise and go the other, what with keeping our eyes open and asking questions, one or other of us is pretty certain to lay hold of him. We can't afford to lose him."

They could not afford to lose Smike indeed, for the work that Smike did—both in the house and in the stable—would have cost the Squeers ten or twelve shillings a week in the shape of wages to any one else.

Mrs Squeers's plan was adopted without a moment's delay; and, after a very hasty breakfast, Squeers started off in the pony-chaise, while Mrs Squeers, arrayed in a white top-coat and tied up in various shawls, went forth in another direction, taking with her a good-sized bludgeon, several pieces of strong cord and a stout labouring man.

Nicholas remained behind in a tumult of feeling, wondering, with an aching heart, where so helpless a creature could have wandered. He lingered on in restless anxiety until the evening of the next day, when Mr Squeers returned alone and unsuccessful.

"No news of the scamp," said the schoolmaster. "Here's the pony run right off his legs, and me obliged to come home with a hack cob, that'll cost fifteen shillings. Who's to pay for that—eh, Nickleby?"

Nicholas shrugged his shoulders, and remained silent.

Another day came, and Nicholas was scarcely awake, when he heard the wheels of a chaise approaching the house. It stopped. And the voice of Mrs Squeers was heard speaking in great triumph.

Nicholas hardly dared to look out of the window. But he did so; and the very first object that met his eyes was the wretched Smike, bedabbled with mud and rain, haggard, worn, and wild.

"We tied his legs under the apron," said Mrs Squeers, "and made 'em fast to the chaise, to prevent him giving us the slip again."

With hands trembling with delight, Mr Squeers unloosened the cord; and Smike, to all appearance more dead than alive, was brought into the house, and securely locked up in the cellar.

The news that Smike had been caught ran like wildfire among the boys. But it was not till the afternoon that Squeers made his appearance in the schoolroom. He was accompanied by Mrs Squeers.

"Each boy keep his place," said Mr Squeers, rapping his desk with his cane. "Nickleby, to your desk, sir!"

There was a very curious expression in the new teacher's face; but he took his seat without making any reply. Squeers then left the room, and shortly afterwards returned, dragging Smike by the collar.

The boys moved uneasily in their seats, and a few of the boldest ventured to steal looks at each other full of indignation and pity.

"Have you anything to say?" demanded Squeers, giving his right arm two or three flourishes. "Stand a little out of the way, Mrs Squeers, my dear. I've hardly got room enough."

"Spare me, sir!" cried Smike.

"Oh! that's all, is it?" said Squeers. "Yes, I'll flog you within an inch of your life—and spare you that."

"I was driven to do it," said Smike faintly, casting an imploring look about him.

"Driven to do it, were you?" said Squeers. "Oh! it wasn't your fault. It was mine, I suppose—eh?"

"A nasty, pig-headed, ungrateful, sneaking dog!" exclaimed Mrs Squeers, taking Smike's head under her arm, and cuffing it. "What does he mean by that?"

"Stand aside, my dear," replied Squeers "We'll try and find out."

Mrs Squeers stood aside. Squeers caught the boy firmly in his grip; one desperate cut had fallen on his body, when Nicholas, suddenly starting up, cried, "Stop!" in a voice that made the rafters ring.

"Who cried stop?" said Squeers, turning savagely round.

"I," said Nicholas, stepping forward. "This must not go on"

Aghast at the boldness of the interference, Squeers released his hold of Smike, and, falling back a pace or two, gazed at Nicholas with looks that were positively frightful.

"I say must not," repeated Nicholas, nothing daunted. "Shall not!—I will prevent it."

Squeers continued to gaze upon him, with his eyes starting out of his head; but astonishment had actually, for the moment, left him speechless.

"You have returned no answer to the letter in which I begged forgiveness for him," said Nicholas. "Don't blame me for this public interference. You have brought it upon yourself"

"Sit down, beggar!" screamed Squeers, almost mad with rage, and seizing Smike as he spoke.

"Wretch!" rejoined Nicholas fiercely. "Touch him at

your peril! I will not stand by and see it done. Look to yourself; for, by Heaven, I will not spare you, if you drive me on."

"Stand back!" cried Squeers, brandishing his weapon.

"Have a care," returned Nicholas; "for if you do raise the devil within me, the consequences shall fall heavily upon your own head."

With a cry like the howl of a wild beast, Squeers spat upon him, and struck him a blow across the face with his cane.

Smarting with the agony of the blow, and filled with rage and indignation, Nicholas sprang upon him, wrested the weapon from his hand, and, pinning him by the throat, beat the ruffian till he roared for mercy.

The boys—with the exception of Master Squeers, who, running to his father's help, kicked Nicholas behind—moved not hand or foot. But Mrs Squeers, with many shrieks for aid, hung on to the tail of her husband's coat, and tried to drag him from the infuriated Nicholas; while Miss Squeers, who had been peeping through the keyhole, darted in, and flung a shower of inkstands at the teacher's head.

Nicholas, feeling that his arm was growing weak, threw all his remaining strength into half-a-dozen finishing cuts, and flung Squeers from him with all the force he could muster. The violence of her husband's fall knocked Mrs Squeers completely over a form close by; and Mr Squeers, striking his head against it as he fell, lay at full length on the ground, stunned and motionless.

Stopping only to make sure that the schoolmaster was

not dead, Nicholas left the family to restore him, and, first looking round for Smike, who was nowhere to be seen, he retired to the sleeping-room.

Here he packed up a few clothes in a small leathern valise; and, finding that no one tried to stop him, he marched boldly out by the front door, striking into the road which led to Greta Bridge. London was two hundred and fifty miles away; but to London he must go, and he had only four shillings and a few pence in his pocket.

Lifting up his eyes, he beheld a horseman coming towards him, whom he discovered, to his great vexation, to be no other than John Browdie, who, clad in cords and leather leggings, was urging his steed forward by means of a stout ash sapling.

"I am in no mood for more noise and riot," thought Nlcholas. "And yet, do what I will, I shall have a quarrel with this honest blockhead."

For John Browdie no sooner saw Nicholas advancing, than he reined in his horse, and waited for Nicholas to come up.

"Weel, we ha' met at last," observed John, making his stirrup ring under a smart touch of his ash stick.

"Yes," replied Nicholas, hesitating. "Come!" he said frankly, after a moment's pause; "we parted on no good terms the last time we met. It was my fault, I believe; but I had no idea of offending you. Will you shake hands?"

"Shake hands!" cried the good-humoured Yorkshireman. "Ah! that I weel." And, bending down from the saddle, he gave Nicholas's fist a huge wrench.

"But wa'at be the matther wi' thy face, mun? It be all broken-loike."

"I have been ill-treated. That is the fact," said Nicholas.

"Noa!" said John. "Dean't say thot."

"Yes, I have," replied Nicholas, "by that man Squeers, and I have beaten him soundly, and am leaving this place in consequence."

"What!" cried John Browdie, with such a delighted shout that the horse quite shied at it. "Beatten the schoolmeasther! Ho! ho! ho! Beatten the schoolmeasther! Who ever heard the loike of that, noo? Giv' us thee hond agean, yoongster. Beatten the schoolmeasther! Dang it, I loov' thee for't."

So saying, John laughed, and laughed again, and shook Nicholas by the hand no less heartily. Then he inquired what Nicholas meant to do. And Nicholas answered that he was going to walk to London.

"Gang awa' to Lunnun afoot!" cried John, in amazement. "Hoo much cash hast thee gotten?"

"Not much," said Nicholas, colouring; "but I can make it enough."

Without a word, John put his hand into his pocket, pulled out an old purse, and insisted that Nicholas should borrow from him whatever he required. "Dean't be afeard, mun," he said. "Tak' eneaf to carry thee whoam."

Nicholas could not be prevailed upon to borrow more than a sovereign, though John entreated him to take more.

"Tak' that bit o' timber to help thee on wi', mun," he added, pressing his stick on Nicholas. "Keep a good heart, and bless thee. Beatten the schoolmeasther! Ecod, it's the best thing a've heerd this twonty year!" And, without waiting to hear the thanks that Nicholas poured forth, John Browdie, still laughing, set spurs to his horse, and rode away.

Nicholas watched the horse and rider out of sight, and then set forward on his journey. He did not travel far that afternoon, and slept that night at a cottage where beds were let at a cheap rate; and, rising early next morning, he made his way before night to Boroughbridge.

Here, within a couple of yards of the roadside, he came upon an empty barn, in a warm corner of which he stretched his weary limbs, and soon fell asleep.

When he awoke next morning, he sat up, rubbed his eyes, and stared. What was that motionless object in front of him?

"Am I dreaming?" cried Nicholas. "And yet am awake—Smike!"

The form moved—rose—advanced—and dropped upon its knees at his feet. It was Smike, indeed.

"Why do you kneel to me?" said Nicholas, raising him.

"To go with you—anywhere—to the world's end", replied Smike, clinging to his hand. 'Let me, oh, do let me! You are my home—my kind friend— take me with you, pray."

"I am a friend who can do little for you," said Nicholas kindly. "How came you here?"

He had followed him, it seemed; had never lost sight of him the whole way.

"I will be your faithful, hard-working servant," said Smike. "I will indeed. I want no clothes," added the poor creature, drawing his rags together. "I only want to be near you."

"And you shall," said Nicholas. "And the world shall deal with you as it does by me. Come!"

With these words, Nicholas strapped his valise on his shoulders, and, taking his stick in one hand, held out the other to his delighted charge. And so they passed out of the old barn together.

7

On the Tramp

In the garret of a tall, meagre house in a tumbledown street in London, Newman Noggs had his home. And on the first floor of the same house lodged Mr and Mrs Kenwigs.

It was the anniversary of the Kenwigses' wedding-day, and they had invited Newman to a little supper-party.

The supper was just over, and the hot punch placed upon the table, when a hasty knock was heard at the room door, and another lodger looked in, in his nightcap.

"Don't be alarmed," said he. "It's Mr Noggs that's wanted."

"*Me!*" said Newman, much astonished.

"Why, it is a queer hour, isn't it," replied the lodger; "and they are queer-looking people, too— all covered with rain and mud. Shall I tell them to go away?"

"No," said Newman, rising. "People?—How many?"

"Two," answered the newcomer.

Newman, muttering that he would be back directly, hurried away. He was as good as his word, for, in an exceedingly short time, he burst into the room, and, seizing a lighted candle from the table, and a tumbler of hot punch, darted away like a madman. He bore his prize straight to his own back-garret, where, footsore and nearly shoeless—wet, dirty, and jaded—sat Nicholas and Smike.

Newman's first act was to compel Nicholas to swallow half of the hot punch at a breath, and his next to pour the remainder down the throat of Smike. "You are wet through," said Newman, passing his hand over the coat that Nicholas had thrown off; "and I—I—haven't even a change," he added, with a wistful glance at the shabby clothes he wore himself.

"I have dry clothes in my bundle," replied Nicholas. "If you look so distressed to see me, you will add to the pain I feel already at being compelled, for one night, to cast myself on you for shelter."

Newman then bustled about, insisted that Nicholas should change his clothes, and that Smike should put on his—Newman's—solitary coat, which he persisted in stripping off for the purpose. And, as Nicholas had still a little of John Browdie's money left, a supper of bread and cheese, some cold meat, and a pot of porter were soon got from the nearest cook's shop.

"Mr Noggs," said Nicholas—as, supper over, they drew near to the fire— "what has my uncle heard from Yorkshire?"

Newman opened and shut his mouth several times, but no sound came from it.

"What has he heard?" urged Nicholas, colouring. "I am prepared to hear the very worst." And, in a few words, he told Newman exactly what had passed at Dotheboys Hall.

"My dear young man, I am proud to hear it," said Newman. And he hit the table a violent blow, as if he had mistaken it for the ribs of Mr Squeers. Then he took, from an old trunk, a sheet of paper which appeared to have been scrawled over in great hask.

"The day before yesterday," said Newman, "your uncle received this letter. I took a hasty copy of it while he was out." And he read as follows:—

DOTHEBOYS HALL,
Thursday Morning

'SIR,—My pa requests me to write to you, the doctors considering it doubtful whether he will ever recover the use of his legs which prevents him holding a pen.

"We are in a state of mind beyond everything, and my pa is one mask of brooses both blue and green, likewise two forms are steeped in his Goar. We were kimpelled to have him carried down into the kitchen where he now lays. You will judge from this that he has been brought very low.

"When your nevew that you recommended for a teacher had done this to my pa, he assaulted my pa with dreadful violence. The monster, having, sasiated his thirst for blood then ran away, taking with him a boy of desperate caracter. Hoping to hear from you when convenient, "I remain,

'Yours and cetrer,
'FANNY SQUEERS.'

A deep silence succeeded the reading of this letter, during which Newman Noggs gazed, with a kind of comical pity, at the boy of desperate character.

"Mr Noggs," said Nicholas, "I must go out at once. I must go to Golden Square. I must see Mr Ralph Nickleby."

"Hear me speak," said Newman, planting himself before Nicholas. "He is away from town. He will not be back for three days. And I know that letter will not be answered before he returns. Its contents are known to nobody but himself and us."

"Are you certain?" demanded Nicholas. "Not even to my mother and sister? Then I will go there; I must see them."

"Now be advised by me," said Newman. "Make no effort to see even them, till he comes home. Do not seem to have been tampering with anybody. When he returns, go straight to him, and speak as boldly as you like."

"You mean well to me," replied Nicholas, after some consideration. "Well, let it be so." And, from sheer fatigue, he presently fell asleep.

The next morning Nicholas secured a small backroom on the second floor, and then made his way to a register office in the hope of getting a situation of some kind. He was not successful, however, and with a sad heart Nicholas retraced his steps homewards.

On the third day Mr Ralph Nickleby returned to Golden Square, and Newman informed Nicholas that it was Ralph's intention to visit Mrs Nickleby and Kate that very day, to give them his own account of Nicholas's behaviour at Dotheboys Hall.

"Then," said Nicholas, "I will meet him there."

Ralph arrived at the dingy house in Thames Street

first, and had just finished reading Miss Squeers's letter to the astonished ladies.

"This is pretty," said Ralph, folding up the letter; "very pretty. I recommend him—though I was convinced he would never do any good—to a man with whom, having behaved himself properly, he might have remained, in comfort, for years. What is the result? Conduct for which he might be imprisoned at the Old Bailey."

"I never will believe it," said Kate indignantly. "Never! It is some base conspiracy."

"My dear," said Ralph, "these are not inventions. Mr Squeers is assaulted; your brother is not to be found. This boy of whom they speak goes with him —remember that."

"It is impossible," said Kate. "Nicholas!—Mamma, how can you sit and hear such statements?"

"I never could have believed it!" sobbed Mrs Nickleby.

"It would be my duty, if he came in my way, to deliver him up to justice," said Ralph; "my bounden duty. Do innocent men steal away from the sight of honest folk, and skulk in hiding-places like outlaws? Do innocent men entice nameless vagabonds, and prowl with them about the country? Assault, riot—what do you call there?"

"A lie!" cried a voice, as the door was dashed open, and Nicholas came into the room.

In the first moment of surprise, Ralph fell back a few paces, quite taken off his guard at this unexpected apparition. Then he stood with folded arms, and looked at his nephew with a scowl, while Kate threw herself between the two.

"Dear Nicholas!" cried Kate, clinging to her brother. "Be calm; consider—"

"Consider, Kate!" cried Nicholas, clasping her hand so tight that she could scarcely bear the pain. "When I consider all, and think of what has passed, I need be made of iron to stand before him."

"Oh, dear, dear!" cried Mrs Nickleby, "that things should have come to such a pass as this!"

"Who speaks in a tone, as if I had done wrong and brought disgrace on her?" said Nicholas, looking round.

"Your mother, sir," replied Ralph.

"Whose ears have been poisoned by you," said Nicholas "by you who heaped every insult, wrong, and indignity upon my head; you who sent me to a den where base cruelty runs wanton, where the lightness of childhood shrinks into the heaviness of age. I call Heaven to witness that I have seen all this, and that you know it."

"Tell us what you really did," said Kate, "and show that these stories are untrue."

"Of what does he accuse me?" said Nicholas.

"First, of attacking your master," put in Ralph.

"I interfered," said Nicholas, "to save a miserable creature from the vilest cruelty. In so doing, I inflicted such punishment upon the wretch, as he will not readily forget."

"You hear?" said Ralph, turning to Mrs Nickleby.

"Oh, dear me!" cried Mrs Nickleby, "I don't know what to think; I really don't."

"Do not speak just now, mamma, I entreat you," said Kate. "About this boy, dear Nicholas, in whose company they say you left?"

"The boy, a helpless creature, made silly from brutality and hard usage, is with me now."

"You hear?" said Ralph. "Everything proved, even upon his own confession. Do you choose to restore the boy, sir?"

"No, I do not," replied Nicholas. "Not to the man from whom I took him."

"Then I say," snarled Ralph, "that this wilful, disorderly fellow shall not have one penny of my money, or one crust of my bread, to save him from the gallows. I will not meet him, nor hear his name. I will not help him, nor those who help him. Of what I meant to do for you, ma'am, and my niece, I do not say a word. And, as I will not ask you to renounce him, I can see you no more."

"I know you have been very good to us," sobbed Mrs Nickleby, "and meant to do a good deal for my dear daughter. But I can't, you know, brother-in-law, I can't renounce my own son. So we must go to rack and ruin, Kate, my dear."

"Stay," said Nicholas, as Ralph turned to go. "You need not leave this place, sir, for it will be relieved of my presence in one minute; and it will be long before I darken these doors again."

"Nicholas," cried Kate, throwing herself on her brother's shoulder, "do not say so. You will break my heart. Mamma, speak to him. Do not mind her, Nicholas."

"I never meant to stay among you, Kate," said

Nicholas tenderly. "Be a woman," he whispered proudly, "and do not make me one while *he* looks on. Love, you will be helped when I am away. I am no help to you—no protector. I should bring you nothing but sorrow and want. Do not keep me here, but let me go at once. There!—Dear girl—dear girl!"

The grasp which had detained him loosened, and Kate fainted in his arms. Nicholas stooped over her for a few seconds, and, placing her gently in a chair, left her to her mother, and was gone.

He reached his poor room, where, no longer borne up by the excitement which had hitherto sustained him, he threw himself on the bed, and gave free vent to his tears.

He had not heard anybody enter, and was unconscious of the presence of Smike, until, happening to raise his head, he saw him standing at the upper end of the room, looking wistfully towards him.

"Well, Smike?" said Nicholas, as cheerfully as he could.

The lad laid his hand timidly on that of Nicholas. "I know you are unhappy," he said, "and have got into trouble by bringing me away. You—you are not rich; you have not enough for yourself, and I should not be here. I tried to go away today, but the thought of your kind face drew me back." And the poor fellow's eyes filled with tears.

Nicholas grasped him heartily by the shoulder. "I would not lose you now, Smike, for all the world could give. You are my only comfort and stay. Give me your hand. My heart is linked to yours. We will journey from this place together, before the week is out."

Nicholas was as good as his word, and, having raised a small sum of money by selling a few of his spare clothes, they started off—Smike with the bundle on his shoulder, and Newman Noggs accompanying them a little way.

"Why won't you tell me where you are going?" urged Newman.

"Because I scarcely know myself," answered Nicholas. "Depend upon it, I will write soon. I shan't forget my best friend."

They walked on for a couple of hours. Then Newman, with many affectionate farewells, retraced his steps towards Golden Square.

"Smike," said Nicholas, as they tramped on alone, "we are bound for Portsmouth. I am young and active, and could be useful in many ways. So could you."

"I hope so," replied Smike, with sparkling eyes. "When I was—you know where—I could milk a cow and groom a horse with anybody. And I am very willing."

"God knows you are," rejoined Nicholas. "Let me have that bundle now! Come!"

"No, no," replied Smike. "Don't ask me to give it up to you."

"Why not?" asked Nicholas.

"Let me do something for you, at least. You will never know how I think day and night of ways to serve you."

"I should be a blind and senseless beast not to see that," said Nicholas. "Smike, I want to ask you a question. Have you a good memory?"

"I could remember when I was a child," answered Smike; "but that is very long ago. I was always confused and giddy at that place you took me from."

"Who was with you when you first went to Yorkshire?"

"A man—a dark, withered man," answered Smike. "I was glad to leave him. I was afraid of him. But they made me more afraid of them, and used me harder too."

"Do you remember no kind woman who hung over you once, and kissed you, and called you her child?"

"No," said the poor creature, shaking his head; "no—never."

"Nor any house but that house in Yorkshire?"

"No," rejoined the poor lad, with a melancholy look. "I remember I slept in a room—a large, lonesome room at the top of a house, where there was a trapdoor in the ceiling. I have covered my head with the clothes often not to see it, for it frightened me— a young child with no one near at night; and I used to wonder what was on the other side. I have never forgotten that room."

It was, by this time, an hour before noon, and bright sunshine lighted up the green fields on either hand. The sheep-bells were music to their ears. And, full of hope, they pushed on with renewed vigour.

Towards evening they reached Godalming, and here they hired two humble beds. The next morning they began their tramp again, and kept onward with steady purpose; but twilight had already closed in when they paused at the door of a roadside inn, yet twelve miles from Portsmouth.

A glance at the toil-worn face of Smike determined Nicholas, and he made up his mind to stay there for the night.

8

Mr Vincent Crummles

The landlord led them into the kitchen, and Nicholas asked what he could give them for supper.

"I'll tell you what," answered the landlord. "There's a gentleman in the parlour that's ordered a hot beefsteak pudding and potatoes at nine. There's more of it than he can manage; so I'll go and ask him if you can sup with him."

"No, no," said Nicholas, holding him back. "I—I am travelling in a very humble manner; and the gentleman may not care for my company

'Lord love you!" interrupted the landlord. "It's only Mr Crummles. *He* isn't particular."

"Is he not?" asked Nicholas, thinking of the beefsteak pudding.

"Not he," replied the landlord. "Wait a minute." And he hurried into the parlour. In two seconds he was back again. "All right," he said, in a low voice. "I knew he would. You'll see something rather worth seeing in there. Ecod, how they are a-going it!"

And, as he had already thrown open the door of the parlour, Nicholas, followed by Smike with the bundle on his shoulder, was obliged to enter.

At the upper end of the room were a couple of boys, one of them very tall, the other very short, both dressed as sailors—or, at least, as theatrical sailors—with belts, buckles, pigtails, and pistols complete—fighting, what is called in playbills, a terrific combat.

"Mr Vincent Crummles," said the landlord, addressing a large, heavy man, who was looking on, "this is the young gentleman."

Mr Vincent Crummles received Nicholas with a bow something between the courtesy of a Roman emperor and the nod of a pot-companion. "There's a picture!" said Mr Crummles, pointing to the boys. "The little 'un has him. If the big 'un doesn't knock under in three seconds, he's a dead man. Do that again, boys!"

The two combatants went to work afresh, and chopped away until the swords sent out a shower of sparks. Then the short sailor closed with the tall sailor, who, after a few struggles, went down and appeared to die in tortures, as the short sailor put his foot upon his breast.

"That'll be a double *encore*, if you take care, boys," said Mr Crummles. "You had better get your wind now, and change your clothes."

"What did you think of that, sir?" inquired Mr Vincent Crummles.

"Very good indeed—capital!" answered Nicholas.

"I open at Portsmouth the day after tomorrow," said Mr Crummles. "If you're going there, look into the theatre, and see how that'll tell"

Nicholas promised to do so if he could, and, drawing a chair to the fire, fell into conversation with Mr

Crummles, who, he soon learned, was a theatrical manager.

Mr Crummles talked a great deal of the merits of his company, and of the cleverness of his own family, looking, from time to time, with great interest at Smike, who had fallen asleep in his chair.

"Excuse my saying so," said the manager, leaning over to Nicholas, "but what a capital countenance your friend has got!"

"Poor fellow!" said Nicholas, with a half smile. "I wish it were a little more plump, and less haggard."

"Plump!" exclaimed Mr Crummles. "You'd spoil it for ever! Why, as he is now, he'd make such an actor for the starved business as was never seen in this country. Only let him be pretty well up in the Apothecary in *Romeo and Juliet*, and he'd be certain of three rounds the moment he appeared on the stage."

And the Apothecary, in Shakespeare's play of *Romeo and Juliet*, is a poor starved-looking man, full of wretchedness and misery.

As the manager spoke, the beefsteak pudding came in, and so did the young Master Crummleses; and the conversation turned to other matters. Indeed, they were all so hungry, that there was no time for talking till supper was over; and then Smike and the Master Crummleses became so sleepy, that the manager suggested they should go to bed, while he and Nicholas had a snug talk by the fire.

Nicholas himself was too anxious to feel sleepy, and sat on, hardly listening to Mr Crummles, who smoked hard, and told a variety of stories, mostly connected with the stage.

"Come," said the manager, seeing presently that Nicholas's attention wandered; "you're uneasy in your mind. What's the matter?"

Nicholas told him that he was anxious to get something to do that would keep himself and his poor fellow traveller, and added, "I shall try for a berth in some ship. There is meat and drink there, at all events."

"Can you think of no other profession that a young man of your appearance could take up easily" asked the manager.

"No," said Nicholas, shaking his head.

"Why, then, I'll tell you of one," said Mr Crummles, throwing his pipe into the fire. "The stage!"

"The stage!" echoed Nicholas, in astonishment.

"The theatrical profession," said Mr Vincent Crummles. "I am in the theatrical profession; my wife is in the theatrical profession; my children are in the theatrical profession. I had a dog that lived and died in it from a puppy. My chaise-pony goes on in *Timour the Tartar*. I'll bring you out, and your friend too. I want a novelty."

Nicholas's breath was almost taken away by this sudden proposal. "I never acted a part in my life," he said, "except at school."

"You'll do as well as if you had thought of nothing else but the stage from your birth upwards," said Mr Crummles. "You can be useful to us in a hundred ways. Think what capital bills a man of your education could write for the shop windows."

"Well, I think I could manage that department," said Nicholas, with a brightening face.

"To be sure you could," replied Mr Crummles. "Do you understand French?"

"Perfectly well," said Nicholas.

"You could turn French plays into English, then," cried the delighted manager. "Capital!"

"What should I get for all this?" inquired Nicholas, after a little thought. "Could I live by it?"

"Live by it!" echoed the manager. "Like a prince! With your own salary, and your friend's, and your translations, you'd make—Ah! you'd make a pound a week!"

"You don't say so!" cried Nicholas.

"I do indeed; and, if we had a run of good houses, nearly double the money."

Without any more hesitation, Nicholas declared that it was a bargain, and gave Mr Vincent Crummles his hand upon it then and there.

The next morning the pony was brought out of the inn stables and harnessed to a four-wheeled phaeton. Nicholas and the manager took the front seat, while the Master Crummleses and Smike were packed together behind.

"The pony is quite one of us," said Mr Crummles, as they jogged along. "His mother was on the stage."

"Was she?" rejoined Nicholas.

"She ate apple-pie at a circus for upwards of fourteen years," said Mr Crummles; "fired pistols, and went to bed in a nightcap. His father was a dancer. He used to drink port wine with the clown; but he was greedy, and one night bit off the bowl of the glass, and choked himself; and that was the death of him."

When they arrived at the drawbridge at Portsmouth, Mr Crummles pulled up. "We'll get down here," said he; "and the boys will take the pony round to the stable."

Nicholas jumped out, and he and Smike accompanied the manager up High Street on their way to the Portsmouth Theatre. Turning by-and-by into an entry, they groped their way through a dark passage, and emerged upon the stage of the theatre.

"Here we are," said Mr Crummles.

And then Nicholas saw, sitting at a small table at the part of the stage in front of the drop-scene, a stout, portly lady in a faded, silk cloak, with her bonnet dangling by the strings in her hand.

"Mr Johnson," said the manager; (for Nicholas had given that as his name), "let me introduce Mrs Vincent Crummles."

"I am very glad to see you, sir," said Mrs Vincent Crummles in a deep voice, shaking Nicholas very heartily by the hand. "You, too, are welcome, sir," she added to Smike.

"He'll do, I think, my dear," said the manager, alluding to Smike.

"He is admirable," said the lady.

As she spoke, there bounded on to the stage from a side door, a little girl in a dirty white frock, with tucks up to the knees, short trousers, sandalled shoes, pink gauze bonnet, green veil, and curlpapers. She turned a pirouette, then—looking at the opposite wing—shrieked, bounded forward to within six inches of the footlights, and fell into a beautiful attitude of terror, as a shabby gentleman, in an old pair of buff slippers, came on, chattering his teeth, and fiercely brandishing his stick.

"They are practising the Indian Savage and the Maiden," said Mrs Crummles.

"Oh!" said the manager. "Very good. Go on."

The Savage then became ferocious, and, after chasing the Maiden into corners, began at last to relent. Then he had a dance all alone, and then the Maiden dancet alone, and after that they both danced together. Then the Savage dropped down on one knee, and the Maiden stood on one leg upon the other knee.

"Very well indeed," said Mr Crummles. "Bravo!"

"This, sir," said Mr Vincent Crummles, bringing the Maiden forward— "this is the infant phenomenon, Miss Ninetta Crummles."

"Your daughter?" inquired Nicholas.

"My daughter," replied Mr Vincent Crummles. "The idol of every place we go into, sir."

"I am not surprised at that," said Nicholas. "She must be quite a natural genius."

"Sir," said Mr Crummles, "the talent of this child is not to be imagined. She must be seen to be appreciated, sir. There! go to your mother, my dear."

Then the Savage came up, and Mr Crummles introduced him as Mr Folair. After that other actors and actresses belonging to Mr Crummles's company appeared on the stage; and in good time all were introduced to "Mr Johnson."

Mr Crummles then gave a roll of paper to Nicholas, containing a French play. "There!" said he; "just turn that into English, Mr Johnson, and put your name on the title-page."

Nicholas pocketed the play; and then Mr Crummles's elder son went with Mr Johnson to show where lodgings were to be had; and Nicholas secured two small rooms over a tobacconist's shop.

"There, Smike," said he, when they were alone, "put our belongings down. We have fallen upon strange times, and Heaven only knows the end of them."

Nicholas worked away at the French piece, which was soon ready for rehearsal; and then he worked away at his own part, which he studied with great perseverance, and acted—as the whole company said—to perfection. And, at length, the great day arrived.

Miss Snevellicci, the chief actress, and the infant phenomenon played their parts so well, that the audience waved their hats and handkerchiefs, and uttered shouts of "Bravo!" But when Nicholas came on for his crack scene with Mrs Crummles as his mother, what a clapping of hands there was! When he fell down on one knee to ask her blessing, how the ladies in the audience sobbed! His air, his figure, his walk, his look—everything he said or did was highly praised.

In short, the success both of the new piece and the new actor was complete. The play was announced for every evening of performance until further notice. And on the following Saturday Nicholas received from Mr Crummles no less a sum than thirty shillings.

The weeks glided busily by, and the company were now rehearsing *Romeo and Juliet*. Nicholas had been chosen to play the part of Romeo; Smike, that of the Apothecary.

"I don't know what's to be done, Smike," said Nicholas anxiously, the evening before the great day. "I'm afraid you can't learn it, my poor fellow." For though, as the Apothecary, Smike had only a few sentences to say, he had been as yet quite unable to get the part into his head.

"I am afraid not," said Smike, shaking his head. "Yet, if you were to keep saying it to me in little bits, over and over again, I think I should be able to recollect it from hearing you."

"Do you think so?" exclaimed Nicholas. "Well said! Now then!— *'Who calls so loud?'*"

"*'Who calls so loud?'*" said Smike.

"*'Who calls so loud?'*" repeated Nicholas.

"*'Who calls so loud?'*" cried Smike.

And so they went on; and when Smike had this by heart, Nicholas went to another sentence, and then to two at a time, and so on, until at midnight poor Smike found, to his unspeakable joy, that he really began to remember something of his part.

Early in the morning they went at it again, and Smike got on faster and faster. Nicholas then showed him how he must come in with both hands spread out upon his stomach, and how he must occasionally rub it, to show that he wanted something to eat.

Never had a master a more anxious, humble pupil. Never had a pupil a more patient, kind-hearted master. They worked on until it was time to go to the theatre. And even there, when he himself was not upon the stage, Nicholas made Smike repeat his part.

They prospered well. The Romeo was received with

hearty favour, and Smike was pronounced, alike by audience and actors, the very prince of apothecaries.

This unexpected success induced Mr Crummles to prolong his stay at Portsmouth, during which time Nicholas acted other parts, and attracted so many people to the theatre, that a benefit was considered, by the manager, a very promising speculation.

The benefit was had: that is, a performance the proceeds of which went entirely to Nicholas, who received no less a sum than twenty pounds.

Nicholas's first act was to return the sovereign to John Browdie, with many grateful thanks; and next he sent to Newman Noggs the sum of ten pounds, begging him to give it to Kate with her brother's best love.

Nicholas said nothing of the way in which he had earned it, merely telling Newman that a letter addressed to Mr Johnson at the Post Office, Portsmouth, would readily find him, and entreating him to write and tell him how his mother and sister were faring, and what Ralph Nickleby had done for them.

"You are out of spirits," said Smike, on the night after the letter had been despatched

"I was thinking about my sister, Smike."

"Sister!" echoed Smike. "Is she like you?"

"Why, so they say," replied Nicholas, laughing— "only a great deal handsomer."

"She must be *very* beautiful," said Smike, with his eyes bent upon his friend. "Shall I ever see your sister?"

"To be sure," cried Nicholas. "We shall all be together one of these days—when we are rich, Smike." And the evening after that a letter came from Newman Noggs.

Newman had sent back the ten pounds, saying that he had found out that neither Mrs Nickleby nor Kate was in actual want of money at the moment. He entreated Nicholas not to be alarmed at what he was about to say: there was no bad news; but he thought it necessary that Kate should have her brother's protection, and that Nicholas should return to London as soon as possible.

Nicholas tossed, sleepless, on his bed that night, thinking incessantly of Kate, filled with the idea that Kate, in the midst of some great trouble, was at that very moment looking—and looking in vain—for him. What could have happened?

"Smike," said he, as soon as the dawn broke, "here— take my purse. Put our things together, and pay what little debts we owe; quick, and we shall be in time for the morning coach. I will tell Mr Crummles that we are going, and will return to you immediately."

Mr Crummles was in despair, and implored Nicholas to stop one more night.

"Not an hour—not a minute," replied Nicholas. "Here, take my hand, and with it my hearty thanks. Goodbye, goodbye!" And Nicholas was gone.

Smike had made good speed, and had everything ready for their departure. Snatching a morsel of breakfast, they arrived in good time at the coach office to secure their places; and, in a few minutes more, they were off.

9

"Who is this Boy?"

They reached London that night, and Nicholas, engaging beds for himself and Smike at the inn where the coach stopped, went without delay to the lodgings of Newman Noggs.

There was a fire in Newman's garret, and a candle had been left burning, and meat and drink were placed in order upon the table for the travellers; but Newman himself was not there.

One of the lodgers informed Nicholas, that Mr Noggs had some troublesome business, which would keep him away till twelve o'clock, and had left word that they were to go on with supper.

Nicholas was much too uneasy to care for supper; so, after he had seen Smike comfortably placed at the table, he started off for the dingy house in Thames Street, to see his mother.

Mrs Nickleby was out, the servant said, and would not be home till late. Miss Nickleby did not live at home now, only coming there very seldom. She couldn't say where she was stopping, but it was not at Madame Mantalini's—she was sure of that.

With his heart beating violently, and fearing he knew

not what, Nicholas returned to Newman's garret, and Newman himself ran out.

"Tell me all," said Nicholas, grasping his hand. "Tell me everything."

"Yes, I will—I will," said Newman. "I'll tell you the whole truth." And, leading Nicholas to the fireside, Newman did so.

He told how, shortly after Nicholas had left London, Madame Mantalini had failed in business and become bankrupt, and how Kate had secured another post, as companion to a Mrs Wititterly, of Cadogan Place, Sloane Street.

How Kate had met there a bold and bad man, named Sir Mulberry Hawk, and his friend Lord Frederick Verisopht. How these two men had persisted in forcing their attentions on beautiful Kate, and had insisted on following her wherever she went.

How Kate, in despair, had at last gone to Ralph Nickleby's house in Golden Square, to beg her uncle's protection, and how taken aback she was at the richness and splendour of Ralph's house—the handsome furniture, the elegant carpets, the exquisite pictures, and all the beautiful and luxurious things in the wealthy money-lender's home.

How Newman—fearing that Kate was in trouble — had listened outside the door, and how he had heard nearly all their conversation. How Kate had said that her uncle was the only friend she had at hand, and how she implored him to save her from these men.

How Ralph had coolly replied, that he was connected in business with Sir Mulberry Hawk and Lord Frederick

Verisopht—indeed, he was constantly lending them large sums of money at enormous interest—and that he could not afford to offend them by interfering in his niece's behalf.

How Kate had walked proudly out of Ralph's room, and how, when she was alone with Newman in the grand hall, she had broken down and cried bitterly. How, almost directly after that, Nicholas's letter had arrived, and how Newman had written at once to tell Nicholas to come back as soon as possible.

Such was the story that Nicholas heard, his blood boiling as he listened, and his hands clenched. "My mother shall not stay another day in that house of Ralph Nickleby's," he said.

And he arranged with Newman that, while he himself should go next morning to Mrs Wititterly's, Newman should go first to Miss La Creevy, to ask her to let Mrs Nickleby and Kate have their old rooms, and then go to Thames Street to prepare Mrs Nickleby for the removal.

Smike and he then returned to the inn, where Nicholas, before going to bed, wrote a few lines to his uncle.

He was up next morning at seven; and, looking into Smike's room to tell him that Newman Noggs would call for him very shortly, Nicholas left the inn, and, calling a hackney coach, bade the man drive to Mrs Wititterly's.

It wanted a quarter to eight when they reached Cadogan Place; and Nicholas, fearing that no one might be stirring at that early hour, was relieved to see a servant cleaning the doorsteps. She told him that Kate was then taking her morning's walk in the gardens before the house.

"Tell her that her brother is here," said Nicholas, "and in great haste to see her."

Soon he heard a light footstep that he knew well, and, before he could advance to meet her, Kate had fallen on his neck and burst into tears.

"My darling girl!" said Nicholas, as he embraced her. "How pale you are!"

"I have been so unhappy here, dear brother," sobbed poor Kate. "Do not leave me here, dear Nicholas, or I shall die of a broken heart."

"I will leave you nowhere," answered Nicholas— "never again, Kate. It is such bitter reproach to me to know what you have undergone. You must leave here with me directly."

And Mr Wititterly, happening to walk into the room at that moment, Nicholas told him what he purposed to do. And, with a hasty apology for so sudden a departure, he hurried Kate into the coach, and bade the man drive with all speed to Thames Street.

Newman Noggs had not been idle, for there was a little cart at the door, and Mrs Nickleby's belongings were being hurried out already.

Mrs Nickleby was in a state of great bewilderment, and could hardly understand such hasty proceedings though good Miss La Creevy had arrived too, and had done her best to explain.

"My dear mother," said Nicholas, "after the discovery of Ralph Nickleby's vile behaviour, you should not be indebted to him one hour longer, even for the shelter of these walls."

"To be sure," said Mrs Nickleby, crying bitterly; "he

is a brute and a monster. I never could have believed it—never."

"Nor I—nor anybody else," returned Nicholas. "Come, mother, there is a coach at the door, and until Monday, at all events, we will return to our old quarters."

"Where everything is ready, and a hearty welcome into the bargain," put in Miss La Creevy.

Then Nicholas got them all into the coach, and away they drove; while he remained behind to see everything safely out. Then he discharged the servant, locked the door, and found his way to a by-place near Golden Square, where he had appointed to meet Newrnan Noggs, to whom he delivered the key and the letter he had written the night before to Ralph.

When Newman reached the office, he laid the key upon the desk, and waited impatiently for the money-lender. Soon he heard his boots creaking on the stairs, and then the bell rang.

"Any letters?" said Ralph.

"One." And Newman laid it on the desk.

"What's this?" asked Ralph, taking up the key.

"Left with the letter. A boy brought them a quarter of an hour ago." And Newman retired.

Ralph opened the letter, and read as follows:—

"You are known to me now. Your brother's widow and her orphan child spurn the shelter of your roof, and shun you. Your kindred renounce you, for they know no shame but the ties of blood which bind them in name with you."

Ralph Nickleby read these lines twice. He recognised Nicholas's writing, and, frowning heavily, fell into a fit of musing.

Presently Newman Noggs entered the room. He was followed by a man and a little boy.

"Why, this *is* a surprise!" said Ralph, who still held the letter in his hand. "I should know your face, Mr Squeers."

"Ah!" replied the schoolmaster—for it was he indeed—"and you'd have knowed it better, sir, if it hadn't been for all that I've been a-going through. My son, sir, little Wackford. What do you think of him, sir, for a specimen of the Dotheboys Hall feeding? Ain't he fit to burst out of his clothes?"

"He looks well, indeed," returned Ralph "But how is Mrs Squeers, and how are you?"

"Mrs Squeers, sir," said the schoolmaster, "is as she always is—a joy to all them as knows her."

"Have you quite recovered that scoundrel's attack?" asked Ralph

"I've only just done it, sir. I was one blessed bruise," said Squeers, touching first the roots of his hair, and then the toes of his boots—"from *here* to *there*. Vinegar and brown paper, vinegar and brown paper, from morning to night.

"Are you stopping at your old quarters?"

"Yes, we are at the Saracen's Head, and shall continue to stop there till I've collected the money, and some new boys, I hope. I've brought little Wackford to show to parents and guardians. Look at that boy —why, he's a miracle of high feeding, that boy is!"

"I should like to have a word with you," said Ralph suddenly.

"As many as you like, sir," rejoined Squeers. "Wackford, you go and play in the back-office. You haven't such a thing as twopence, Mr Nickleby, have you?" said Squeers, rattling a bunch of keys in his coat pocket, and muttering something about its being all silver.

"I—think I have," said Ralph very slowly, and producing, after much rummaging in an old drawer, a penny, a halfpenny, and two farthings.

"Thankee," said Squeers, giving it to his son. "Here! you go and buy a tart. Mr Nickleby's man will show you where—and mind you buy a rich one. Pastry," added Mr Squeers, closing the door on Master Wackford, "makes his flesh shine, and parents thinks that a healthy sign."

"Attend to me," said Ralph, bending towards him. "You are not dolt enough to forgive or forget the violence that was committed upon you?"

"Not I," replied Squeers tartly.

"Who is this boy that he took with him? Speak out."

"A young fellow named Smike, nigh twenty years old. He wouldn't seem so old, though, to them as didn't know him; for he was a little wanting here," added Squeers—tapping his forehead. "It's fourteen years ago, by the entry in my book, since a strange man brought him to my place, and left him there, paying five pound five for his first quarter in advance. He might have been five or six year old at that time—not more. The money was paid for some six or eight year, and then it stopped; and I could never find out anything about the chap that brought him. So I kept the lad out of—out of—"

"Charity?" suggested Ralph drily.

"Charity, to be sure," returned Squeers "And when he begins to be useful in a certain sort of way, this young scoundrel of a Nickleby comes and carries him off."

"We will both cry quits with him before long," said Ralph, laying his hand on the arm of the schoolmaster.

"Quits!" echoed Squeers "I only wish Mrs Squeers could catch hold of young Nickleby. She'd murder him, sir."

"If," muttered Ralph, almost to himself, "if I could strike him through his affection for this boy."

"Strike him how you like, sir," interrupted Squeers. "Only hit him hard enough. And with that I'll say good morning.—Here! just chuck that little boy's hat off that corner peg—will you?"

Bawling this request to Newman Noggs, Mr Squeers betook himself to the little back-office, where Newman, with his pen behind his ear, sat stiffly on his stool, regarding the father and son by turns with a broad stare.

"He's a fine boy, ain't he?" said Squeers.

"Very," said Newman.

"Pretty well swelled out, ain't he?" went on Squeers. "He has the fatness of twenty boys, he has."

"Ah!" replied Newman, suddenly thrusting his face into that of Squeers, "he has;—the fatness of twenty!—More! He's got it all. God help the others!—Ha! ha!"

"Why, what does the man mean?" cried Squeers, colouring. "Is he drunk?"

But Newman was bending over his desk, writing with marvellous rapidity.

"He *is* drunk," said Squeers. And, with this parting observation, he led his son away.

Having established his mother and sister in the apartments of the kind-hearted Miss La Creevy, Nicholas went in search of Smike, who, after breakfasting with Newman Noggs, had remained at Newman's lodgings, waiting, with much anxiety, for Nicholas.

"I was afraid," said Smike, overjoyed to see his friend again, "that you had fallen into some trouble. I almost feared you were lost."

"Lost!" replied Nicholas gaily. "You will not be rid of me so easily. Come. My errand is to take you home."

"Home!" faltered Smike, drawing timidly back.

"Ay," rejoined Nicholas, taking his arm. "Why not?"

"I had such hopes once," said Smike. "But now—"

"And what now?" asked Nicholas kindly.

"I am a poor creature," faltered Smike. "I know that."

"Why, here's a dismal face for ladies' company! My pretty sister, too, whom you have so often asked me about. Is this your Yorkshire gallantry? For shame! For shame!"

Smike brightened up and smiled.

"When I talk of home," went on Nicholas, "I talk of mine—which is yours, of course—the place where those I love are gathered together. Come." And, taking his companion by the arm, and talking kindly, Nicholas led the way to Miss La Creevy's.

"And this, Kate," said Nicholas, entering the room where his sister sat alone— "this is the faithful friend and affectionate fellow-traveller whom I have prepared you to receive."

Poor Smike was frightened and awkward enough at first; but Kate advanced to him so kindly—and said, in such a sweet voice, how much she had to thank him for having comforted Nicholas in his trying times—that he managed to say, in a broken voice, that Nicholas was his only friend, and that he would lay down his life to help him.

Then Miss La Creevy came in; and to her Smike had to be presented too; and Miss La Creevy talked so merrily, and made so many small jokes, that Smike thought, within himself, she was the nicest lady he had ever seen.

At length the door opened again, and a lady in mourning came in, and Nicholas, kissing her affectionately, led her towards Smike.

"You are always kind-hearted, and anxious to help the oppressed, my dear mother," said Nicholas, "so you will be favourably disposed towards my friend, I know."

"Any friend of yours," answered Mrs Nickleby cordially, "has a great claim upon me." And, then, she had so much to say, both to her son and to her daughter, that poor Smike recovered from his bashfulness, and soon felt quite at home.

10

New Friends and Old Enemies

Nicholas knew that, with his mother and sister depending on him, it would be impossible now for him to seek a livelihood upon the stage; and he knew, too, that his slender stock of money would be soon gone.

"Egad!" said Nicholas, "I'll try that register office again;" and he walked away with a quick step. The office looked just the same as when he had left it last; and, as he stopped to look in at the placards in the window, an old gentleman happened to stop too.

He was a sturdy old fellow in a broad-skirted blue coat, with no particular waist. His bulky legs were clothed in drab breeches and high gaiters, and he wore a low-crowned, broad-brimmed white hat. And he had such a clear, twinkling, honest, merry eye, and such a pleasant smile, that Nicholas was emboldened to speak.

"A great many opportunities here, sir," said Nicholas, motioning to the placards in the window.

"A great many people anxious to be employed have thought so, I dare say," replied the old man.

He moved away as he said this; but, seeing that Nicholas was about to speak again, he good-naturedly turned back. "What were you going to say, young gentleman?"

"Merely," hesitated Nicholas, "that I almost hoped you had some object in looking at these advertisements."

"What object now?" replied the old man, looking slily at Nicholas. "Did you think I wanted a situation—eh? Did you think I did?"

Nicholas shook his head.

"Ha! ha!" laughed the old gentleman. "I thought the same of you at first; upon my word, I did."

"If you had thought so at last, too, sir, you would not have been far from the truth," returned Nicholas.

"Eh!" cried the old man. "What! No, no. Well-behaved young gentleman reduced to such a necessity! What d'ye mean—eh?"

With that he put his hand on the shoulder of Nicholas, and walked him up the street. "You're in mourning, eh? Who's it for?"

"My father," replied Nicholas.

"Ah!" said the old gentleman quickly. "Bad thing for a young man to lose his father. Widowed mother, perhaps?"

"Yes," said Nicholas.

"Brothers and sisters too—eh?"

"One sister," replied Nicholas.

"Tell me your history," said the old gentleman. "Let me hear it all." There was something so earnest and simple in the way in which this was said, that Nicholas could not resist it; and he presently found himself telling his little history without reserve.

"Don't say another word," said the old gentleman, when Nicholas had finished; "not another word. Come along with me. We mustn't lose a minute." So saying, he hailed an omnibus on its way to the City, pushed Nicholas in before him, and followed himself. And whenever Nicholas attempted to speak, he stopped him with, "Don't say another word, my dear sir—not another word."

He got out when they reached the Bank, and, once more taking Nicholas by the arm, hurried him along Threadneedle Street, until they came to a quiet little square; and into one of the houses of business here he led the war. On the door-post was printed CHEERYBLE BROTHERS; and, from a hasty glance at the directions of some packages lying about, Nicholas supposed that the brothers were London merchants trading with Germany.

Passing through a warehouse full of busy porters, the old gentleman led him into a little partitioned-off counting-house, in which there sat a fat, elderly, large-faced clerk, with silver spectacles and a powdered head.

"Is my brother in his room, Tim?" said Mr Cheeryble.

"Yes, he is, sir," replied the fat clerk.

At that, Mr Cheeryble led Nicholas to the half-opened door of another room, and tapped with his knuckles, saying, "Brother Ned, can you spare time for a word or two with me?"

"Brother Charles, my dear fellow," replied a voice from inside, "come in directly."

They went in. And what was the amazement of Nicholas, when his conductor exchanged a warm greeting with another old gentleman the very type and model of himself—the same face, the same figure, the same coat, waistcoat, breeches, and gaiters—nay, there was the very same white hat hanging against the wall. Nobody could have doubted that they were twin-brothers.

"Brother Ned," said Nicholas's friend, closing the door, "here is a young friend of mine whom we must assist. We must make proper inquiries into his statements, of course, and if they are confirmed—as I feel assured they will be—we must assist him, brother Ned."

"What are his necessities, and what does he require?" asked Brother Ned. "Where is Tim Linkinwater? Let us have him here."

"Stop, stop!" said Brother Charles, taking the other aside. "I've a plan, my dear brother, I've a plan. Tim is getting old; and if we could lighten Tim's duties, old Tim Linkinwater would grow young again in time. But first, let me tell you this young gentleman's history. It will affect you, Brother Ned; and you will remember the time when we were two friendless lads, and earned our first shilling in this great city." And in his own homely way Brother Charles related the story he had heard from Nicholas.

The conversation which followed was a long one, and, when it was over, a private talk took place between Brother Ned and Tim Linkinwater in the other room.

At length, Brother Ned and Tim came back together, and Tim, walking up to Nicholas, whispered that he had taken down his address in the Strand, and would call upon him that evening at eight.

Nicholas's heart was so full, that he could hardly stammer out his thanks, which the old gentlemen would not listen to.

"We will say goodbye for the present," said Brother Ned, shaking his hand.

And Nicholas—almost bewildered at the turn of events—found his way back to Miss La Creevy's.

It is impossible to recount all the delight and wonder his story awakened in the breasts of Mrs Nickleby and Kate, and all the things they said, thought, expected, and hoped.

It is enough to state, that Mr Timothy Linkinwater arrived punctually at eight; that he reported strongly in favour of Nicholas; and that, next day, our hero was appointed to a stool in the counting-house of Cheeryble Brothers, with a present salary of one hundred and twenty pounds a year.

More than that. At Bow—which, in those days, boasted many pretty gardens—a little cottage belonging to Cheeryble Brothers was let to Nicholas at a trifling rent; and, in one short week, Nicholas took possession of the stool at the counting-house, and Mrs Nickleby and Kate took possession of the cottage; and all was hope, bustle, and joy.

Miss La Creevy came out in the omnibus to stop a day or two to help to get the house in order, while Smike made the garden a perfect wonder to look upon.

All the peace and cheerfulness of home was restored; and while the poor Nicklebys at the cottage were friendly and happy, the rich Nickleby in Golden Square was alone and miserable.

They had been settled some three weeks in their new home, when Miss La Creevy came again to see the cottage 'thoroughly got to rights,' as she expressed it, 'from the chimney-pots to the streetdoor scraper'; and it was arranged that Smike was to escort her home.

When they reached her house in the Strand, the good-natured little woman would by no means allow of Smike's walking back again, until he had first been refreshed with a sip of something comfortable, and a mixed biscuit or so; and it fell out that it was after dusk when he set forth on his journey home.

There was no likelihood of his losing his way, for he had walked into the City with Nicholas, and back alone, almost every day; so he stepped out briskly, stopping now and again to gaze in at the window of some particularly attractive shop, and then walking on briskly again.

He had been looking for a long time through a jeweller's window—wishing he could take some of the beautiful trinkets home as a present for Kate— when the clocks struck three-quarters past eight.

Roused by the sound, Smike hurried on at a very quick pace, and was crossing the corner of a bystreet, when he felt himself violently brought to, with a jerk so sudden, that he was obliged to cling to a lamp-post, to save himself from falling.

At the same moment a small boy clung tight round his leg, and a shrill cry of "Here he is, father! Hooray!" sounded in his ears.

Smike knew that voice too well. And, shuddering from head to foot, he looked round.

Mr Squeers had hooked Smike in the coat-collar, with the handle of his umbrella; while Wackford, regardless of all Smike's kicks and struggles, clung to him with the tenacity of a bulldog. Smike himself became utterly powerless, the terrified lad being unable to make a sound.

"Here's a go!" cried Mr Squeers, unhooking the umbrella when he had got tight hold of Smike's collar. "Here's a delicious go! Wackford, my boy, call up one of them coaches."

"A coach, father!" cried little Wackford.

"Yes, a coach, sir," replied Squeers, feasting his eyes upon the countenance of Smike. "Hang the expense! Let's have him in a coach."

"What's he been a-doing of?" asked a labourer, with a hod of bricks.

"Running away, sir," replied Mr Squeers; "joining in blood-thirsty attacks upon his master. Oh, what a delicious go is this here, 'pon my word!"

The man looked from Squeers to Smike; but such wits as poor Smike possessed had utterly deserted him. The coach came up. Master Wackford entered; then Squeers pushed in his prize, and, following close at his heels, pulled up the glasses; and the coachman mounted his box and drove away.

Mr Squeers sat himself down on the opposite seat to the unfortunate Smike, and, after looking at him for some five minutes, uttered a loud laugh, and slapped his old pupil's face several times.

"Your mother will be fit to jump out of her skin, my boy, when she hears of this," said Squeers to his son.

"Oh, won't she, though, father?" replied Wackford.

"To think," said Squeers, "that you and me should be turning out of a street, and come upon him at the very nick; and that I should have him tight, at only one cast of the umbrella Ha, ha!"

"Didn't I catch hold of his leg, neither, father?" said little Wackford.

"You did, like a good 'un, my boy," replied Squeers, patting his son's head. "And you shall have the best button-over jacket and waistcoat that the next new boy brings down, as a reward of merit." And then, in a bantering tone, he asked Smike how he found himself by this time.

"I must go home," replied Smike, looking wildly round.

"To be sure, you must. You're about right there," replied Mr Squeers. "You'll be home very soon, you will. You'll find yourself at the peaceful village of Dotheboys, in Yorkshire, in something under a week's time, my young friend. Where's the clothes you run off in, you ungrateful robber?"

Smike glanced at the neat suit that Nicholas had provided for him, and wrung his hands.

"What do you suppose was the worth of them clothes you had?" went on Squeers—first poking Smike in the chest with the umbrella, and then dealing a shower of smart blows with it upon his head and shoulders. Do you know that it's a hanging matter to walk off with up'ards of the valley of five pound from a dwelling-house?"

Poor Smike! He warded off the blows as well as he could, and shrank into a corner of the coach, with his head resting on his hands and his elbows on his knees, utterly stunned and stupefied.

Mr Squeers now began to thrust his head out of the window every half minute, and to bawl directions to the coachman. And, after passing through several mean streets, the coach stopped before a small house with a brass plate on the door, bearing the name of Snawley.

"Here we are!" said Squeers, hurrying Smike into the little parlour, where Mr Snawley and his wife were taking a lobster supper. "Here's the vagrant— the rebel— the monster of unthankfulness!"

"What! The boy that run away!" cried Mr Snawley — the same Snawley that had placed his two step-sons under Mr Squeers's care, and at whose house Squeers, having left the Saracen's Head, had taken lodgings for a short time.

"The very boy," said Squeers. "I have been, Mrs Snawley, that chap's benefactor, feeder, teacher, clothier. Mrs Squeers has been his mother, grandmother, aunt—ah! and I may say uncle too—all in one."

"Where has he been all this time?" inquired Snawley. "Has he been living with—"

"Ah, sir!" interrupted Squeers, turning on Smike. "Have you been a-living with that there villainous Nickleby, sir?"

But no threats or cuffs could extort from Smike one word of reply to this question; for he had resolved that he would rather be dragged back to his wretched prison than utter one syllable that could hurt his first friend. For Smike had a confused idea that Nicholas might have committed some terrible crime in bringing him away—a crime for which he might be punished heavily.

Finding every effort useless, Mr Squeers at last conducted him to a little back-room upstairs, where he was to pass the night; and, locking the door on the outside, he left Smike to his own thoughts.

What those thoughts were, and how the poor fellow's heart sank within him when he thought of his late home, and the dear faces with which it was associated, cannot be told. And Smike crept to bed, the same listless, hopeless, blighted creature that Nicholas had first found him at the Yorkshire school.

11

John Browdie to the Rescue

The night, laden with so much bitterness to poor Smike, had given place to a bright and cloudless summer morning, when a north-country mail coach came rattling through the streets of London.

Among the passengers was honest John Browdie, who, having been lately married to Miss Price, had come to spend his honeymoon sight-seeing in the great City.

The coach stopped hard by the Post Office, and John, getting down, and opening the coach door, tapped Mrs Browdie on the cheek, and then offered his arm to help out another lady—no other than Miss Fanny Squeers—who, having acted as 'Tilda's bridesmaid, had come to London with the wedding party.

Calling a hackney coach, they drove straight to the Saracen's Head, where they first retired to get some sleep after the long night journey, and met again, about noon, at a substantial breakfast.

They learned from the waiter, that Mr Squeers was not stopping at the inn, but that he came there every day, and that, directly he arrived, he should be shown up into the room.

"Hond up another pigeon pie, will'ee?" said John.

And the waiter had not retired two minutes, when he reappeared with Mr Squeers and little Wackford.

"Why, who'd have thought of this?" said Mr Squeers.

"Who indeed, pa!" replied Miss Squeers. "But you see 'Tilda is married at last."

"Will'ee pick a bit?" inquired John.

"I won't myself," returned Squeers; "but if you'll just let little Wackford tuck into something fat, I'll be obliged to you. What do you think?" added the schoolmaster. "Who do you suppose we have laid hands on, Wackford and me?"

"Pa! Not Mr" Miss Squeers was unable to finish the sentence, but Mrs Browdie did it for her, and added, "Nickleby?"

"No," said Squeers. "But next door to him, though."

"You can't mean Smike?" cried Miss Squeers, clapping her hands.

"Yes, I can, though," rejoined her father. "I've got him, hard and fast."

"Wa'at!" exclaimed John Browdie, pushing away his plate. "Got that poor—awful scoondrel—where?"

"Why, in the top back-room at my lodging," replied Squeers, "with him on one side, and the key on the other."

"At thy loodgin'! Thee'st gotten him at thy loodgin'? Ho! ho! The schoolmeasther agin all England." And, by way of congratulation, John dealt Squeers such a blow on the chest, that the schoolmaster staggered in his chair.

"Thankee," said Squeers. "But don't do it again. You mean it kindly, I know, but it hurts rather. Yes, there he is. It was pretty neatly done, and pretty quick too."

"Hoo wor it?" inquired John, sitting down close to him. "Tell us aboot it, mun. Coom, quick!"

Mr Squeers related the lucky chance by which Smike had fallen into his hands, and added, with a cunning look, "For fear he should give me the slip, I've took three outsides on the coach for tomorrow morning—for Wackford and him and me—and have arranged to leave the accounts, and the new boys to the agent. So it's lucky you come today, or you'd have missed us; and as it is, unless you would come and tea with us tonight, we shan't see anything more of you before we go away."

"Dean't say anoother wurd," returned John. "We'd coom, if it was twenty mile." And he assured Mr Squeers that they would be at Mr Snawley's at six o'clock without fail.

During the rest of the day, Mr Browdie was in a very strange and excitable state, bursting into fits of laughter, and walking restlessly in and out, and behavng so oddly, that Miss Squeers thought he was going mad.

Mrs Browdie, however, was not at all alarmed, and said that she had seen him so once before, and that, although he was sure to be ill after it, it would be nothing very serious, and therefore he was better left alone.

And, indeed, while they were all sitting in Mr Snawley's parlour that night, and, just as it was beginning to get dark, John Browdie was taken so ill, that the whole company were thrown into the utmost consternation.

Mrs Browdie was the only person present that remained calm, and she suggested that if John were allowed to lie down on Mr Squeers's bed for an hour or so, and left entirely to himself, he would be sure to recover almost as quickly as he had been taken ill.

Accordingly, John was supported upstairs with great difficulty being a monstrous weight, and regularly tumbling down two steps every time they hoisted him up three; and, being laid on the bed, he was left in the charge of his wife, who, in a short while, reappeared in the parlour with the good news that he had fallen fast asleep.

Now the fact was that, at that very moment, John was sitting on the bed, with the reddest face ever seen, cramming the corner of the pillow in his mouth to prevent his roaring out loud with laughter.

Presently he slipped off his shoes, and, creeping into the adjoining room where poor Smike was imprisoned, John turned the key which was on the outside, and, darting in, covered the lad's mouth with his huge hand before he could utter a sound.

"Ods-bobs, dost thee not know me, mun?" whispered the Yorkshireman to the bewildered Smike. "Browdie—John Browdie."

"Yes, yes!" cried Smike. "Oh, help me!"

"Help thee!" replied John. "Thee didn't need help, if thou warn't a silly youngster as ever draw'd breath. Wa'at did 'ee come here for, then?"

"He brought me. Oh! he brought me," said Smike.

"Why didn't 'ee punch his head, or lay theeself doon and squeal out for the pollis? I'd ha' licked a dozen such as him when I was as yoong as thee. But thee be'st a poor broken-down chap,' said John sadly; 'and God forgi' me for bragging ower one o' His weakest creeturs! Stan' still," added the Yorkshireman, "and doan't speak a morsel o' talk till I tell 'ee." And, drawing a screwdriver from his pocket, he took off the box of the lock in a very workman-like manner, and laid it, with the screwdriver, on the floor.

"See thot?" said John. "Schoolmeasther'll think thot be thy doing. Noo, foller me, and when thee get'st outside door, turn to the right, and they wean't see thee pass."

"But—but—he'll hear me shut the door," replied Smike, trembling from head to foot.

"Then dean't shut it at all," retorted John. "Dang it, thee bean't afeard o' schoolmeasther's takkin' cold, I hope?"

"N-no," said Smike, his teeth chattering in his head. "But he brought me back before, and will again. He will, he will indeed."

"He wean't—he wean't!" replied John impatiently. "Look'ee, I want to do this neaighbourly-loike, and let them think thee's gotten awa' o' theeself. But if he cooms oot o' thot parlour awhiles thee'rt clearing off, he mun have mercy on his own boans, for I wean't. If thee keep'st a good heart, thee'll be at whoam afore they know thee'st gotten off. Coom!"

The frightened Smike prepared to follow with tottering steps, when John whispered in his ear, "Thee'lt just tell yoong Measther that I'm married to Tilly Price, and to be heerd on at the Saracen by letter." And, gliding downstairs and hauling Smike behind him, John placed himself close to the parlour door, to confront the first person that might come out, and signed to Smike to make off.

Smike needed no second bidding. Opening the front door gently, and casting a look of mingled gratitude and terror at his deliverer, he took the turning to the right, and sped away like the wind.

The Yorkshireman remained at his post for a few minutes, but, finding that there was no pause in the conversation inside, he crept back again unheard, and stood listening over the stair-rail for a full hour. Everything remaining perfectly quiet, John got into Mr Squeers's bed once more, and, drawing the clothes over his head, laughed till he was nearly smothered.

In the meanwhile, without pausing to consider where he was going, Smike fled away with surprising swiftness; and it was not until it had grown very late, that— covered with dust, and panting for breath —he stopped to listen and look about him, and discovered that he was on a country road.

Squeers could hardly trace him by such paths as he had taken; and, turning back, the poor lad made for London again. And, asking his way, from time to time, of the people in the streets, Smike at length reached the dwelling of Newman Noggs.

All that evening Newman had been searching in by-ways for the very person who now knocked at his door; and he was sitting at his poor supper, when Smike's timid knock reached his ears.

Alive to every sound in his anxious state, Newman hurried downstairs, and, uttering a joyful cry of surprise, dragged the welcome visitor up the stairs; and when he had him safe in his own garret, he mixed a great mug full of gin and water, and, holding it to Smike's mouth, commanded him to drain it to the last drop.

Poor Smike did little more than put his lips to the mixture, and then he managed to tell his tale.

"You shall stay here," said Newman. "You are tired— fagged. I'll tell them you're come back. They have been half mad about you. Mr Nicholas—"

"God bless him!" cried Smike.

"Amen!" returned Newman. "He hasn't had a minute's rest or peace. No more has Miss Nickleby."

"No, no! Has she thought about me" said Smike. "Has *she*, thought? Oh!—has she—has she?"

"She has," cried Newman. "She is as noble-hearted as she is beautiful" And he added, "You shall remain here for the night; and I shall go to the cottage to relieve their suspense."

Smike, however, would not hear of this; and the two sallied forth together. But the lad was so footsore, that he could scarcely crawl along; and it was within an hour of sunrise when they reached their destination.

At the first sound of their voices outside the house, Nicholas, who had passed a sleepless night, started from his bed and joyfully admitted them. There was so much noisy conversation, that the remainder of the family were soon awakened; and Smike received a warm welcome, not only from Kate, but from Mrs Nickleby also. And to them his story had to be told again.

Nicholas wrote at once to John Browdie, who, in his turn, wrote and invited Nicholas to tea.

"Aha!" cried John, when the waiter showed Nicholas in. "Thee hond, Mister Nickleby. Hoo be all wi' ye? Ding! But I'm glad o' this."

"You remember the night of our first tea-drinking?" said Nicholas, after greeting young Mrs Browdie.

"Shall I ever forget it, mun?" replied John.

"He was a desperate fellow that night, though, was he not, Mrs Browdie?" said Nicholas. "Quite a monster!"

"If you had only heard him as we were going home, Mr Nickleby, you'd have said so indeed," returned the bride. "I never was so frightened in all my life."

"Coom, coom," said John, with a broad grin; "thou know'st better than thot, Tilly."

"This is the second time," said Nicholas, as they took their places at the table, "that we have ever taken a meal together, and only the third time I have ever seen you; and, yet, it really seems to me, as if I were among old friends. But I can never tell you how grateful that poor lad and I, and others whom you don't know, are to you for taking pity on him."

"Ecod!" rejoined John. "And I can never tell *you* how grateful soom folks would be loikewise, if *they* knowed I had takken pity on him."

"Ah!" exclaimed Mrs Browdie, "what a state was in that night!"

"There I lay," said John, laughing heartily, "snoog in schoolmeasther's bed long after it was dark, and nobody coom nigh the place. 'Weel!' thinks I, 'he's got a pretty good start. And schoolmeasther may come as quick as he loikes.' Presently I heerd a door shut doonstairs, and him a-walking up in the dark. He turns the key, when there warn't nothing to hoold the lock, and ca's oot, 'Hallo, there!'—No answer. 'I'll brak every boan in your boddy, Smike,' says he. Then, all of

a soodden, he sings out for a light, and when it cooms—
ecod! such a hoorly-boorly! 'Wa'at's the matter?' says
I. 'He's gane!' says he, stark-mad wi' vengeance. 'Have
ye heerd nought?' 'Ees,' says I. 'I heerd street door
shut, no time at a' ago. I heerd a person run doon there'
(pointing t'other way). 'Help!' he cries. 'I'll help you,'
says I. And off we set—the wrong wa'! Ha! ha! ha!"

"Did you go far?" asked Nicholas.

"Far!" replied John. "I run him clean off his legs. To
see old schoolmeasther, wi'out his hat, skimming along,
and bawling oot like mad wi' his one eye looking sharp
out for the lad, and his coat-tails flying out behind! I
thot I should ha' killed myself wi' laughing." And John
laughed so heartily at the mere recollection, that
Nicholas and Mrs Browdie were obliged to laugh too;
and all three burst into peals of laughter, and laughed till
they could laugh no more.

"He's a bad 'un," said John, wiping his eyes— "a very
bad 'un is schoolmeasther."

"Miss Squeers is stopping with you, you said in your
note?" remarked Nicholas.

"Yes," replied John. "Tilly's bridesmaid. She wean't
be a bride in a hurry, I reckon."

"For shame, John," said Mrs Browdie. And she added,
"John fixed tonight for you to come to tea, because
Fanny had settled that she would go and see her father.
But do you know, Mr Nickleby, I was given to under-
stand, by Fanny herself, that you two were going to be
engaged quite solemn and regular—"

"Was you, ma'am—was you!" cried a shrill female
voice. "Was you given to understand that I—I—was go-

ing to be engaged to an assissinating feller that shed the gore of my pa?—Oh! base and degrading 'Tilda!" And Miss Squeers flung the door wide open, and disclosed to the eyes of the astonished Browdies and Nicholas, not only herself, but the forms of little Wackford and Mr Squeers.

"This is the *h*end, is it," continued Miss Squeers, "of all my forbearance and friendship for that double-faced thing? This is the *h*end, is it, of my taking notice of that viper, and demeaning myself to patronise her?"

"Oh, come," rejoined Mrs Browdie, "don't talk such nonsense as that!"

"Oh, ma'am, how clever you are!" retorted Miss Squeers, with a low curtsey. "How very clever it was in you to choose a time when I had gone to tea with my pa! What a pity you never thought that other people might be as clever as you, and spoil your plans."

"I don't know that I have said anything very bad of you, Fanny," returned Mrs Browdie. "At all events, what I did say was quite true; but I am very sorry for it, and I beg your pardon."

Miss Squeers looked at her former friend from top to toe, and, raising her nose in the air, muttered the word 'minx.'

Mr Squeers, meanwhile, was scowling at John with a very malicious expression. "It was you, was it," said he, "that helped off my runaway boy?"

"Me!" returned John, in a loud voice. "Yes, it was me. And I'll tell 'ee more If thou'd got twenty runaway boys, I'd do it twenty times ower. And noo that my blood's oop, I tell 'ee that thou'rt an old ra'ascal, and that it's well for thee thou be'st an old 'un, or I'd ha poonded thee to flour, when thou told an honest mun hoo thou'd licked that poor chap in t' coach."

"Scandal!" said Mr Squeers exultingly. "Rascal, eh?" And, taking out his pocket-book, he made a note of it. "Very good. I should say that was worth twenty pound at the next Assizes."

"Soizes!" cried John. "Thou'd betther not talk to me of Soizes. Yorkshire schools have been shown up at Soizes afore noo, mun; and it's a ticklish soobject to revive, I can tell ye."

Mr Squeers shook his head in a threatening manner, looking very white with passion; and, taking his daughter's arm, and dragging little Wackford by the hand, retreated towards the door.

"As for you," said Squeers, turning round and addressing Nicholas, "you'll go a-kidnapping boys, will you? *Take care their fathers don't turn up*, and send 'em back to me, to do as I like with them, in spite of you."

Nicholas only shrugged his shoulders contemptuously; and Squeers turned his back with an evil look; while Miss Squeers, looking loftily round, said scornfully, "I leave such society with my pa for *h*ever!"

12

A Claimant for Smike

Ralph Nickleby was out making calls, and very odd calls he made—some at great rich houses, and some at small poor ones—but all upon one subject: money.

It was evening before his visits were ended, and Ralph walked along St. James's Park on his way home. There were so many deep schemes in his head, that Ralph did not observe that he was followed by the shambling figure of a man, who watched him with eager looks.

The sky had been dark for some time, and a violent shower of rain drove Ralph for shelter to a tree. He was leaning against it with folded arms, when, happening to raise his eyes, he suddenly met those of a man, who, creeping round the trunk, peered into his face, with a searching look.

"Do you remember me, Mr Nickleby?" he said.

Ralph bent upon him a severe look, and saw a dark, withered man, deeply sunburnt, with hollow, hungry cheeks, and recognised the face of a person whom he had had dealings with twenty years ago, and with whom he had fallen out, and made an enemy of some time later.

"I am a most miserable outcast," said the man; "nearly sixty years old—destitute and helpless."

"I am sixty years old too," said Ralph, "and am neither destitute nor helpless. Work, and earn your bread."

"I have a hold upon you," said the man—"a hold that you would give half of all you have to know, and can never know but through me. Fourteen years ago I took advantage of my position about you, and, partly in the hope of making money some day by the scheme, I possessed myself of this hold. For seven years I have been a convict, and have just returned to London. Now, Mr Nickleby—what help will you give me—what bribe, to speak out plainly?"

"Hark ye, Mr Brooker," returned Ralph, in his harshest accents. "I know you of old for a ready scoundrel. You a hold upon me! Keep it; or publish it to the world, if you like."

"That wouldn't serve me," replied Brooker. "I can tell you of what you have lost by my act; what I only can restore; and what, if I die without restoring, dies with me, and never can be regained."

"And I can tell you, 'scape-gallows, that if we meet again, and you so much as notice me by one begging gesture, you shall see the inside of a jail once more. There's my answer. Take it." And, with a disdainful scowl, Ralph walked away.

The dark, withered man remained on the same spot, till the figure of Ralph was lost to sight; then he limped with slouching steps by the wayside, and begged of those that passed along.

Ralph, meanwhile, walked homewards, his thoughts full of his latest plan. "Are they here?" was the first question he asked of Newman.

"Ay," said Newman. "In your room now."

"Get me a coach," said Ralph. And, the coach arriving, there went into it Ralph, Mr Squeers, and a third man, whom Newman had never seen. And, to Newman's astonishment, he heard Ralph tell the coachman to drive to Nicholas's cottage.

"Drive *there*," muttered Newman, as the coach rolled away. "Drive *there!* There's mischief in it."

As he spoke, a dark, withered man approached, and begged for alms. Newman looked into his hat for some halfpence, which he kept screwed up in the corner of a handkerchief; and as he did so, Brooker—for it was he—said something that in interested Ralph's clerk so greatly, that he walked away by the strange man's side, Brooker talking earnestly, and Newman listening.

Now on that very evening Mr and Mrs Browdie had been invited to supper at Nicholas's cottage, and, supper being over, they had just returned to the parlour.

The pretty bride had at first been very bashful in the company of Mrs Nickleby and Kate, but Kate had the art of turning the conversation to subjects upon which the country girl could feel herself at home, and had soon put Mrs Browdie at her ease.

"Mr Browdie," said Kate, addressing the young wife, "is the best-humoured and heartiest creature I ever saw. If I were oppressed with I don't know how many cares, it would make me happy only to look at him."

Suddenly a loud and violent knocking was heard at the street door, and a second later Ralph Nickleby walked into the room.

Nicholas rose, but Kate threw herself upon his arm,

while Smike retreated behind them; and John Browdie, who had heard of Ralph, stepped between the old man and his young friend.

"Before that boy says a word," said Ralph, pointing to Nicholas, "hear me."

"Say what thou'st gotten to say, then, sir," retorted John. "And tak' care thou dinnot put up angry bluid, which thou'dst better try to quiet."

"I should know *you*," returned Ralph, "by your tongue, and *him*" (pointing to Smike) "by his looks."

"I will not hear that man," burst out Nicholas. "Do not speak to him. His presence is an insult to my sister. I will not bear it."

"Stand!" cried John, laying his heavy hand on Nicholas's chest.

"Then let him instantly retire," cried Nicholas, struggling. "I will not have him here. John—John Browdie—is this my house—am I a child?"

But John still kept his hold of Nicholas. "Wa'at be that shadow ootside door there?" said he. "Noo, schoolmeasther, show thyself, mun. Dinnot be sheamfaced."

At that, Mr Squeers, who had been lingering in the passage, sneaked into the room, while Ralph addressed himself to Mrs Nickleby. "I have a motive in coming here," he said. "I come here"—looking round with a triumphant smile— "to restore to a parent his child. Ay, sir," he continued, turning to Nicholas, "to restore to a parent his child—his son, sir—waylaid, and carried off by you. I have his father here."

"Here!" sneered Squeers, stepping forward. "Do you

hear that? Didn't I tell you to be careful *that his father
didn't turn up* and send him back to me? Smike's to
come back to me directly, he is."

"Tell the father," put in Ralph, "that he might now ap-
pear, and claim his own."

Squeers immediately left the room, and returned with
no less a person than Mr Snawley, who, making straight
up to Smike, and tucking that poor fellow's head under
his arm in a most awkward embrace, waved his hat in
the air, exclaiming, "How little did I think of this here
joyful meeting when I saw him last! Oh, how little did I
think it! No wonder my heart yearned towards him."

"It was a parent's instinct, sir," observed Mr Squeers.
"It only shows what Natur' is. She is a rum 'un is
Natur'."

At this moment Smike, escaping from his father, fled
to Nicholas, and implored him never to give him up, but
to let him live and die beside him.

"If you are this boy's father," said Nicholas, "look at
the wreck he is, and tell me that you purpose to send
him back to that loathsome den from which I brought
him."

"Stop," interposed Ralph, as Mr Snawley was about
to speak. "Let us cut this matter short, by proving that
this boy is your son." And he went on to explain, how
Snawley had been separated from his first wife—who
had taken their boy to live with her when he was a year
old. How, a couple of years later, she had written to
Snawley, saying that the boy was dead. And how, when
she herself lay dying only eighteen months ago, she had
written a confession, to the effect—that she had only

pretended that the boy was dead to wound Snawley, who had been very fond of the child. That she had sent him to a cheap school in Yorkshire, and had left him there under the name of Smike. That she had paid for his education for some years, and then, being poor, had gradually deserted him, for which she prayed forgiveness. And that, owing to some strange circumstance, the letter had reached Snawley only three days ago.

"There," ended Ralph, tossing Snawley's pocketbook upon the table, "the certificates of his first marriage and of the boy's birth are there, as well as his wife's two letters. You can examine them, if you like." And, with a smile, Ralph sat down unbidden, folded his arrns, and looked at his nephew.

Nicholas, commanding his feelings as well as he could, looked closely at the papers, which appeared to be quite correct; while Kate, who had been looking anxiously over his shoulder, whispered, "Can this really be the case? Is this statement true?"

"I fear it is," answered Nicholas.

"Well," said Squeers, "what's to be done? Them hackney-coach horses will catch cold if we don't think of moving. Is Master Snawley to come along with us?"

"No, no, no!" cried Smike, clinging to Nicholas. "No. Pray, no. I will not go from you to him. No, no."

"This is a cruel thing," said Snawley. "Do parents bring children into the world for this?"

"Do parents bring children into the world for *thot?*" said John Browdie, pointing, as he spoke, to Squeers.

"Never you mind," retorted the schoolmaster, advancing upon Smike.

"Noo then, where be'est thou comin' to?" cried John. "Dinnot coom treadin' ower me, mun!" And Mr Browdie jerked his elbow into the chest of Mr Squeers, with so much dexterity, that the schoolmaster staggered back upon Ralph, and knocked that gentleman off his chair.

In the commotion that followed, an attempt was made to carry off the lost son by violence, and, notwithstanding the entreaties of Smike, and the loud cries of the women, Squeers had actually begun to haul him out, when Nicholas took the schoolmaster by the collar, and, thrusting him into the passage, shut the door upon him.

"Now," said Nicholas to the other two— "have the goodness to follow your friend."

"I want my son," said Snawley.

"Your son," replied Nicholas, "chooses to remain here, and he shall."

"You are an unnatural, ungrateful boy," said Snawley, turning to the terrified Smike. "You won't let me love you when I want to."

"He never loved nobody," bawled Squeers through the keyhole. "He never loved me. He never loved Wackford, who is next door but one to a cherubim."

Mr Snawley looked steadfastly at his son, and then, covering his eyes with his hand, walked sadly out.

"Your romance is destroyed, sir," said Ralph, lingering a moment. "He is not"—pointing to Smike— "the persecuted son of a man of high degree, but the weak, imbecile boy of a petty tradesman." And, with a triumphant smile, Ralph Nickleby withdrew.

Nicholas could not help feeling that he was in a very

perplexing position, and, finding himself alone the next morning with Brother Charles, he related all Smike's little history.

"You are surprised," said Brother Charles, "that I have listened to your story with so little astonishment. That is easily explained. Your uncle has been here this morning. He has told me all. But you shall not be wronged, my dear sir. Nobody belonging to you shall be wronged. I have seen the father—if he is the father—and I suppose he is. He is a barbarian and a hypocrite, Mr Nickleby; and we must keep cool."

13

Smike is Happy

"Noggs," said Ralph Nickleby a few days later, "what man was that whom I saw you with in the street last night?"

"I don't know," returned Newman. "He came here twice, and asked for you. He gave the name of Brooker."

"What—then?" said Ralph.

"Why, then he lurked about and dodged me in the street. He follows me night after night, and urges me to bring him face to face with you."

"He is an idle ruffian," said Ralph; "a swindler, who has the audacity to try his schemes on me. The next time he tampers with you, hand him over to the police—d'ye hear?"

"I hear," said Newman.

And now Ralph Nickleby, having been foiled in his attempt to make Nicholas give up Smike, was planning to thwart his nephew in another way.

It happened that the Cheeryble Brothers were greatly interested in a beautiful young girl named Madeline Bray, whose spendthrift father had wasted all his fortune, and who now spent on himself all that his devoted daughter earned by painting; and to help her, the good Brothers had often employed Nicholas to buy these paintings for them at a high price.

Another money-lender named Arthur Gride, who had business dealings with Ralph, had got into his possession a Will by which Madeline Bray was entitled to certain property which—if the existence of this Will ever became known to her—would make the man she married rich and prosperous.

It fell out that the Will was stolen by an old serving-woman of the money-lender; and Arthur Gride in his despair and wrath—for he had hoped to gain by it himself—disclosed the secret to Ralph Nickleby; and Ralph, to serve his own purpose, suggested to Squeers that Squeers should get hold of this Will to prevent Nicholas from profiting by it, should he ever marry Madeline Bray; for Ralph suspected— and rightly suspected—that Nicholas was getting attached to the beautiful girl.

"I want that Will brought here," said Ralph, "that I may give the man that brings it a hundred pounds in gold."

"One hundred pound is five boys," thought Squeers, "and five boys takes a whole year to pay a hundred pound." And as he was quite ready to thwart Nicholas, and as Ralph told him where he should most likely find the old woman, who, of course, would have no suspicion of Squeers, the schoolmaster agreed to try to secure the Will.

During these days Smike had become paler and thinner, more haggard, and more worn. The poor fellow had never recovered the horror of his capture by Squeers;

and the still greater horror of being claimed by Snawley was wearing the lad away.

And now Smike became so alarmingly ill, that he could scarcely move from room to room without assistance; and the doctor told Nicholas that the last chance of his life depended on his being instantly removed from London, and recommended, as the most favourable spot, Dawlish, in Devonshire, which happened to be the very place where Nicholas had spent his boyhood.

The kind Brothers insisted that Nicholas should take Smike away at once. And the very next morning they started on their journey.

"See," cried Nicholas, looking out of the coach window, "they are at the corner of the lane still. And there's Kate! waving her handkerchief. Don't go without waving to Kate."

"I cannot do it!" cried his trembling companion, falling back in his seat. "Do you see her now? Is she still there?"

"Yes, yes!" said Nicholas earnestly. "There! she waves her hand again. Now they are out of sight. Do not give way so bitterly, dear boy. You will see them all again."

"In heaven," whispered Smike, raising his thin hands, and clasping them fervently. "I humbly pray to God—in heaven."

They procured a quiet lodging in a small farmhouse, surrounded by meadows, where Nicholas had often played as a child. And here they took up their rest. By night and day, at all times and seasons, Nicholas never left him, and never tired in his self-imposed duty to one so friendless and helpless.

There was an old couch in the house, which was the dying boy's favourite resting-place by day; and when the sun shone, Nicholas had this wheeled into a little orchard that was close at hand; and, Smike being well wrapped up, and carried out to it, they used to sit there sometimes for hours together.

One morning, as they sat there, Nicholas, who had watched the whole of the night before, and was greatly fatigued, gradually fell asleep. He could not have closed his eyes five minutes, when he was awakened by a scream, and, starting up in terror, saw, to his astonishment, that Smike had struggled into a sitting posture, and, with the cold dew standing on his forehead, was calling to him for help.

"Good Heaven, what is this?" said Nicholas, bending over him. "Be calm. You have been dreaming."

"No, no, no!" cried Smike, clinging to him. "Hold me tight! Don't let me go! There—there—behind the tree!"

Nicholas followed his eyes, but there was nothing there. "This is nothing but your fancy," he said. "Nothing else, indeed."

"I know better," answered Smike. "I saw as plain as I see now. Oh! say you'll keep me with you. Swear you won't leave me for an instant."

"Do I ever leave you?" returned Nicholas. "Lie down again—there! Now tell me—what was it?"

"Do you remember," said Smike, glancing fearfully round, "my telling you of a man who first took me to the school?"

"Yes, surely."

"I raised my eyes, just now, towards that tree— that one with the thick trunk—and there, with his eyes fixed on me, he stood!"

"Do you think," said Nicholas, "that, at this distance of time, you could possibly know that man again?"

"Anywhere—in any dress," returned Smike. "He stood leaning upon his stick—a dark, withered man — and looking at me exactly as I told you I remembered him."

Nicholas tried to convince the terrified boy that he had been dreaming, but all in vain. And though he succeeded in calming the fears of Smike, the lad declared, in the most solemn manner, that he had really seen what he had described.

And now Nicholas began to see that hope was gone; that Smike was wasted to the last degree. There was little pain, little uneasiness, but there was no struggle for life; and Smike had laid him down to die.

On a fine, mild autumn day, when all was tranquil and at peace, Nicholas sat in his old place by the bedside, and knew that the time was come. The boy had been asleep, when, suddenly, the closed eyes opened, and on the pale face there came a placid smile.

"I have had such pleasant dreams," said he; "such pleasant, happy dreams."

"Of what?" asked Nicholas.

The dying boy put his arm about his friend's neck, and whispered, "I shall soon be there."

After a short silence he spoke again. "I am not afraid to die," he said. "I am quite contented. You have so often told me we shall meet again, that I can even bear to part from you."

"You say well," answered Nicholas, "and you comfort me very much, dear fellow. Let me hear you say you are happy, if you can."

"I am happy," murmured Smike.

They embraced, and kissed each other on the cheek; and Smike fell into a light slumber, and, waking, smiled as before. Then he spoke of beautiful gardens, which, he said, were filled with figures of men, women, and many children—all with light upon their faces; then whispered that it was Eden —and so died.

14

"All Up with Squeers"

In the meanwhile Squeers, when he had agreed to try
and secure the Will, did not know that he was followed
by Newman Noggs, who, as he could not himself keep a
watch on Squeers, enlisted the services of a young
nephew of the Cheeryble Brothers, to follow Squeers's
movements.

Frank Cheeryble undertook the task with all his heart,
and was so successful in his watch on Squeers, that
Squeers had no sooner got possession of the Will, than
Frank Cheeryble, with the help of Newman and a police
officer, got possession of Squeers.

"Noon, and Noggs not here!" said Ralph Nickleby.
"This is strange. What keeps him away? I would give
something to be rid of that fellow; for he is a traitor, I
swear."

As he thought thus, his housekeeper looked in to say
that Mr Charles Cheeryble had called and left a message, saying that he wished to speak with Mr Nickleby,
at his office in the City.

Ralph received the message in a contemptuous manner, and scorned to comply with it. But as he sat on, he
grew strangely ill at ease; and his anxiety increased as

the time passed and no Newman arrived. Then he left home, and slowly made his way to the offices of Cheeryble Brothers.

"Gentlemen," said he, "I wish to know what you have to say to me."

"Brother Ned," said Brother Charles, "will you ring the bell?"

The bell was rung; the room door opened; a man came in; and, looking round, Ralph's eyes met those of Newman Noggs. And from that moment his heart began to fail him.

"Mr Nickleby," said Brother Charles, "Mr Noggs has learned that Smike is not the son of the man Snawley."

"I shall make him prove that," retorted Ralph.

"The proof is ready to our hands," returned Brother Charles. "Snawley last night made a confession. He confessed that the letters declared to have been written by his first wife were forgeries, and that Mr Ralph Nickleby had helped to write them."

Ralph's hardened manner did not change; his features did not move a muscle.

"Squeers," went on Brother Charles, "is in custody, having been taken with a stolen document in his pocket. And justice must take its course against those concerned in the plot to injure a poor unoffending boy. Mr Nickleby, we would not have an old man like you punished by his near relation; we therefore entreat you to retire from London, to take shelter in some place where you will be safe from the consequences of these wicked schemes."

"And do you think," said Ralph, rising, "you will so easily crush *me*? Do you think that a hundred false witnesses will move *me?* I thank you for disclosing your plans, which I am now prepared for; and I taunt you to do your worst."

He left the Brothers, and, throwing himself into a coach, drove to the police office, finding there Mr Squeers, in a kind of waiting-room, where he had been allowed to pass the day, before being taken to prison.

"Why have you not sent for me?" said Ralph "How could I come until I knew what had befallen you?"

"Here's a shock for my family!" said Squeers. "The coat-of-arms of the Squeerses is tore, and their sun is gone down in the ocean wave."

"You have been drinking," said Ralph; for there was a strong smell of brandy-and-water in the room, and an empty glass was on the table, and the schoolmaster's nose was very red.

"I haven't been drinking *your* health, my codger," replied Squeers. 'Prisoner,' says the magistrate to me, 'as you were detected in possession of this document, I shall remand you for a week, that inquiries may be made.' "I will hand in my card," went on Squeers. "I will say, I was merely employed by my friend Mr Ralph Nickleby, of Golden Square. Send for him, sir—he's the man; not me!"

"What document was it you had?" asked Ralph.

"Why, *the* document," replied Squeers. "The Madeline What's-her-name one—The *Will*."

"Beaten at every point," muttered Ralph.

"Ah!" sighed Squeers, upon whom the brandy-and-water was taking effect; "at the delightful village of Dotheboys, near Greta Bridge, in Yorkshire, youth are boarded, clothed, booked, washed, instructed in all languages—here's a altered state of things, this is! A double l—all, everything—a cobbler's weapon. U-p—up, adjective, not down. S-q double e r-s, noun substantive, a educator of youth. Total, all up with Squeers."

Ralph left him. "This fellow, I plainly see," he said, "has made up his mind to turn upon me. I am beset and hemmed in. But they shall not move me," muttered Ralph. "I will not budge an inch."

He went home, and was glad to find his housekeeper complaining of illness, so that he might have an exccuse for being alone and sending her away; and he sat down with his head upon his hand, filled with a strange sense of desolation.

It was nearly ten o'clock when he heard a knocking at his door, and he roused himself to go downstairs.

"Mr Nickleby, there is terrible news for you. I am sent to beg that you will come with me directly. I have a coach here." And Ralph saw, upon the steps, Tim Linkinwater.

Tim said afterwards, that Ralph reeled and staggered like a drunken man, and looked at him with a face so ashy pale, that it made him shudder. Not a word was said during the drive; and Ralph followed his conductor into a room where the Brothers sat.

"What—what have you to say to me," he said, "more than has been said already?" The room was very dimly lighted; and, casting his eyes towards the bay window, he thought he saw the dusky figure of a man. "Who's that yonder?" he asked.

"One who has brought to us the news which caused us to send for you," said Brother Charles.

"Well, sir?" said Ralph faintly.

"What if we tell you," said Brother Ned, "that the poor, unfortunate boy, sinking under your persecution,—and under the misery of a life short in years but long in suffering—has gone to tell his tale where—for your part in it—you must surely answer?"

"If you tell me that he is dead," said Ralph, "I forgive you all else. I would have travelled a hundred miles afoot to hear this news just at this time. And *he* brought you the news—did he?" added Ralph, pointing with his finger to the bay window. "Ha, ha, ha!"

"You take me for your nephew," said a hollow voice. and the figure that he had so dimly seen came slowly forward.

Ralph started back. He was seen to tremble; for he saw—not Nicholas, as he had supposed, but Brooker.

"That boy," said the darkc, withered man, "whom I saw stretched dead and cold upon his bed"—Brooker raised his eyes and clasped his hands solemnly together— "that boy *was your own son*, so help me God in heaven!"

In the midst of an awful silence Ralph sat down, pressing his two hands upon his temples; while Brooker, looking away from Ralph, and addressing the Brothers, spoke in a humble tone.

He told how, twenty years ago, Ralph had secretly married a lady entitled to a large property—a lady who—as her father's will declared—should lose the property, if she married without her brother's consent.

When their little boy was born, he was put out to nurse a long way off, and his mother visited him only by stealth. She lived a wretched life; and when they had been married seven years, she quarrelled with her husband and left him.

Ralph followed to bring her back; but she died before he found her. Before he went, he had entrusted to Brooker the charge of bringing back the little boy. And Brooker, taking him to Golden Square, lodged him in the front garret.

Ralph was gone more than six weeks, and Brooker, whom he had used badly, conceived a plan, by which he hoped to have his revenge on Ralph, and afterwards to get money out of him for revealing his secret. He took the boy to a Yorkshire school, and, giving him the name of Smike, left him with a man named Squeers, and when Ralph came home at last, he told him that the child was dead.

"He was grieved at that," went on Brooker. But he had hardly spoken the words, when the lamp, which stood upon the table close to where Ralph was seated, was thrown to the ground, and they were left in darkness.

There was some confusion in getting another light; but when it appeared, Ralph Nickleby was gone.

Shivering from head to foot, Ralph had made his way to his own home. His own child—his own child! He never doubted the tale. He felt that it was true. His own child! And dead, too! Dying beside Nicholas—loving him, and looking upon him as something like an angel. That was the worst! His own son, who might have been a comfort to him, and they two happy together!

After a pause, he groped his way out of the sitting-room, and up the echoing stairs—up to the top—to the front garret—where he closed the door behind him and remained.

They came to look for him next morning—Tim Linkinwater and the Brothers; and, after searching in vain through the big house, they made their way at last to the front garret.

He had torn a rope from one of the old trunks, and hanged himself on an iron hook immediately below the trap-door in the ceiling—in the very place to which the been directed in childish terror, fourteen years before.

The day after the boy's death, Nicholas returned home, and mother and sister mourned with him the death of one whose grateful nature had, every day endeared him to them more and more.

"To look now upon the garden that he took such a pride in," sobbed Mrs Nickleby— "I cannot bear it; I really cannot."

And Miss La Creevy, who had come to see them, no sooner saw Nicholas, than she sat herself down upon the stairs, and, bursting into a flood of tears, refused to be comforted for a long time.

The news of Squeers's downfall had reached Yorkshire; and John Browdie, who had returned to his own home, now learned that Squeers had been sentenced to be transported for seven years, for being in the unlawful possession of a stolen will.

"If this news has reached school today," said John, "the old 'ooman wean't have a whole boan in her boddy; nor Fanny neither."

"Oh, John!" cried Mrs Browdie.

"I dinnot know what they lads mightn't do," said John. "But I think they'll a' gang daft, and spill bluid like wather!"

In fact, John's fears were so strong, that he determined to ride over to the school without delay; and, arriving at Dotheboys Hall, he made his way to the schoolroom door, which he found locked on the inside.

A tremendous noise rose from within, and, putting his eye to a convenient crevice in the wall, he soon learned its meaning.

It was brimstone-and-treacle morning, and Mrs Squeers had entered with the large bowl and spoon, followed by Miss Squeers and Wackford; and their entrance was the signal to revolt.

While one set of boys rushed to the door and locked it, another set mounted on the desks and forms. The strongest boy seized the cane, and, snatching off Mrs Squeers's cap and beaver bonnet, put them on his own head, armed himself with the wooden spoon, and bade her go down upon her knees, and take a dose directly.

Before Mrs Squeers could recover from her astonishment, she was forced into a kneeling position by a crowd of shouting boys, and compelled to swallow a spoonful of the odious mixture—made more savoury by the dipping in the bowl of Master Wackford's head, whose ducking was entrusted to another rebel.

The leader was insisting upon Mrs Squeers repeating her dose, Wackford was undergoing another dip in the treacle, and a violent assault had been begun on Miss

Squeers, when John, bursting open the door with a vigorous kick, rushed to the rescue.

The shouts, screams, groans, hoots, and clapping of hands suddenly ceased, and a dead silence followed.

"Ye be noice chaps," said John, looking steadily round. "Wa'at's to do here, thou yoong dogs?"

"Squeers is in prison, and we're going to run away!" cried a score of shrill voices. "We won't stop, we won't stop!"

"Weel, then, dinnot stop," replied John. "Who waants thee to stop? Run awa' loike men, but dinnot hurt the women."

"Hurrah!" cried the shrill voices, more shrilly still.

"Weel, hurrah loike men, too," went on John. "Noo then, look out Hip-hip-hip-hurrah!"

"Hurrah!" cried the voices.

"Noo then," said John, "let's have one more, and then coot off as quick as you loike. Tak'a good breath noo— Squeers be in jail—the school's brokken oop, it's a' ower—past and gane—think o' thot, and let it be a hearty 'un. Hurrah!"

Such a cheer arose as the walls of Dotheboys Hall had never echoed before; and when the sound had died away, the school was empty.

"Very well, Mr Browdie!" said Fanny Squeers, "you've been and excited our boys to run away. If my pa *is* unfortunate, we're not going to be crowed over by you and 'Tilda."

"Noa!" replied John, "thou bean't. Think betther o' us, Fanny. I tell 'ee both that I'm glod the auld man has been caught at last, but I be not the mun to crow over you, nor be Tilly the lass. I tell 'ee, Fanny, that if thou need'st friends to help thee awa' from this place, thou'lt foind Tilly and me ready to lend thee a hond. And so I say agean, Hurrah! and dang the schoolmeasther—there!" With that John strode heavily out, remounted his nag, and rode away.

For some days afterwards the country round was overrun with boys, who, the report went, had been secretly furnished by Mr and Mrs Browdie not only with a hearty meal, but with sundry shillings to help them on their way; and soon Dotheboys Hall, and its last breaking-up, began to be forgotten by the neighbours.

Nicholas married Madeline Bray, and his first act, when he became a prosperous merchant, was to buy his father's old house at Dawlish, and his children played in the old meadows.

Within a stone's-throw was another retreat, made lively by children's voices too, and this was Kate's happy home, and her husband was young Frank Cheeryble.

There was one grey-haired, quiet, harmless gentleman, who lived in a little cottage hard by, whose chief pleasure and delight was in the children. The little people could do nothing without dear Newman Noggs.

The grass was green above the dead boy's grave and through all the spring and summer time garlands of fresh flowers, made by childish hands, rested on the stone; and when the children came to change them, their eyes filled with tears, as they spoke low and softly of their poor dead cousin.